Name: Anisha Mistry (I do have a middle name but it's too embarrassing so I am **NOT** writing it here)

Age: 10 years, 3 months and 10 days (at time of writing this)

Lives with: Mum, Dad, and my mischievous Granny Jas

School: Birmingham South-West Aspire Junior Middle High Academy School (longest school name ever!)

Favourite Subject: Science

Best friend: Milo Moon

Ambitions: To meet a real life astronaut

To invent a cure for meanness

To be the first kid in space

For teachers everywhere. For everything you do.
SERENA

For my nephew, Arthur, Best Actor in a Musical/Comedy
Golden Globe Winner 2046
EMMA

First published in the UK in 2021 by Usborne Publishing Ltd., Usborne House,
83-85 Saffron Hill, London EC1N 8RT, England, usborne.com

Usborne Verlag, Usborne Publishing Ltd., Prüfeninger Str. 20,
93049 Regensburg, Deutschland VK Nr. 17560

A CIP catalogue record for this book is available from the British Library.

JFMAM JASOND/22 ISBN 9781474989756 8794/1

Printed in India

ANISHA
ACCIDENTAL DETECTIVE

SHOW
STOPPERS!

SERENA PATEL
Illustrated by Emma McCann

USBORNE

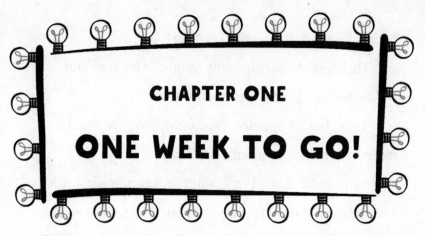

CHAPTER ONE

ONE WEEK TO GO!

I know something is up the moment I hear the special assembly music coming from the hall. Mr Graft only puts on that song "**Reach for the Stars**" when something special is happening. And when we file into the hall that Friday afternoon, I know straight away this is not your average assembly. For a start Miss Jive and Mr Notes, the drama and music teachers, are sitting onstage looking very happy. The big TV screen is on behind them and it says **One Week To Go!**

I turn around and nudge Milo, who is behind me in the line. "One week till what?"

"Maybe they're giving us an extra week off?"

Milo replies. "That would be **cool**!"

"Unlikely, Milo, plus why would Miss Jive and Mr Notes need to be onstage for that?"

"True, but I hope it's something good. We could do with some excitement," Milo says.

My tummy turns. I'm not big on excitement – the last time anything exciting happened in school was when Milo and I got accused of **flooding** the whole place with foam! We all sit down and I look around the hall. It's only our year group in here. What does that mean? We wait as Mr Graft walks to the front of the hall. He looks weird, nervous even.

"Settle down, children. Right, good afternoon, everyone. You might be wondering why we are all here. Well, we have the most **thrilling** news and I hope you will be as happy as we are about this amazing opportunity for our school. I'm going to hand over to Miss Jive and she will tell you all about it."

Miss Jive stands up and smooths her skirt. She steps forward and smiles at us all. "Well, I suppose I should start at the beginning. Our school has been selected to take part in a competition."

ONE WEEK TO GO!

A ripple of whispers and murmurs runs through the hall. Miss Jive clears her throat. "We are one of four schools in the Birmingham area specially selected to take part. Each school has one week to cast, rehearse and put on a musical production." Miss Jive pauses for our reaction. We all look around at each other. Some of the kids seem really **enthusiastic** about the idea – there's already **chatter** about costumes and wondering what the play will be about. One week doesn't sound like very long to do all that, though! And a **musical**?! My first thought is I hope I don't have to sing!

Miss Jive seems to have read my mind. "I know some of you might wonder if it's possible to put on a play in a week, but never fear, we have a plan! We were given a choice of musicals to pick from a hat and this is what we got." She points excitedly to the big screen, which has now changed to show a picture of a man. I recognize him!

"That's Einstein!" I shout out, forgetting we're

supposed to raise our hand.

Miss Jive chuckles. "I thought you would know who this is, Anisha. Yes, you're right. It is indeed Albert Einstein, inventor, scientist and mathematician."

Beena Bhatt, who is unfortunately sitting just a little way in front of me, raises her hand. "Urgh, miss, are we doing a play about maths?"

Miss Jive shakes her head. "No, Beena, maths was just a part of who Einstein was. The musical is actually a lot of fun, showing him in a different light – as a husband, a musician, even a sailor! And did you know his wife Mileva actually helped him a lot with his discoveries? There are some great songs, too. I thought perhaps you might want to play your trumpet?"

Beena goes pink in the face. "Well, I stopped my lessons because I was getting a bit **bored** with it. Too many other interesting things to do, you know how it is."

Miss Jive frowns. "Oh, well that's a shame. You're the only trumpet player we have and I was thinking you'd make a great solo..."

Beena practically **jumps** up, apparently changing her mind completely. "I'll do it!" she shouts. "I mean, if you have no one else and to be honest you need me to make this play cool. Is there another

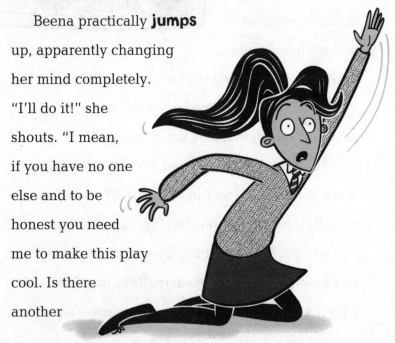

leading part apart from smelly old Einstein? I'd make a great leading lady." She smiles **sweetly**.

Miss Jive looks over at Mr Notes, who rolls his eyes and smiles.

"Well, Beena, I'm not sure we should be referring to Einstein as **old** or **smelly**, but, yes, there is the part of his wife, Mileva," Mr Graft replies.

"I'll do it!" Beena shouts out again.

Miss Jive frowns. "Well, I'm afraid it's not as simple as that. All the acting parts have to be **auditioned** for. Which brings me nicely to the scripts! I'll start passing them back – take one and pass on the pile, everyone."

Beena humphs and sits back down. One of her minions, Layla, leans over to her and whispers, "You've totally got that part, Beena. No one else is as good as you." Beena sits up straighter, pleased with herself.

I look over at Mindy and Manny, who are sitting behind us. Mindy looks deep in thought and Manny is examining something sticky on his finger – I don't want to know what it is.

When the scripts reach me, I take one and pass the rest to Milo. The script is stapled at the top and the front page says **Einstein – not just a scientist!**

Miss Jive signals for us to listen again. "Now, I realize not everyone will want to audition, but I would like you all to read the script over the weekend and get familiar with it. We will need to work together as a **team**, Year Six.

This is a huge project and we only have a week to pull it off. I will need actors, singers, dancers, musicians, scenery and prop makers, make-up artists and backstage help. There will be a role for everyone. Our school has never had this opportunity before, so we want to give it our best shot, don't we? And to help that, all other lessons are cancelled this week. You will be working on the play and only on the play!"

Everyone cheers at that last part.

"What do we win?" someone shouts out.

Miss Jive beams. "Well, it's a really fantastic prize. We would win a huge trophy for our school and one lucky person who displays special talent will win a place on the exclusive summer-school programme at **Dreams Dance and Drama Academy**, the big performing arts school in the city. They have had quite a few of their students go on to work in the West End and even on the telly!" Miss Jive is almost **giddy** now. "The academy will be sending a talent scout to each school's performance and he or she will decide who wins. It's so **exciting**, children, and I would love for one of you to be awarded that place. We have a lot of **talent** in this school and now is your time to **shine**!" She claps her hands together.

I see Beena lean over to Layla, grinning. "That place is mine!" she says.

I stare down at the script in front of me.

A musical. Okay, a musical. It's just some songs and a few scenes, right? And it's about one of my favourite people. So it could be fun...

But I **hate** singing and dancing. I really don't want to perform. And in one week? We'll **never** be ready.

Plus, **drama scouts**? I've never met a scout for anything – it all sounds a bit scary.

The truth is... This is one of my worst nightmares.

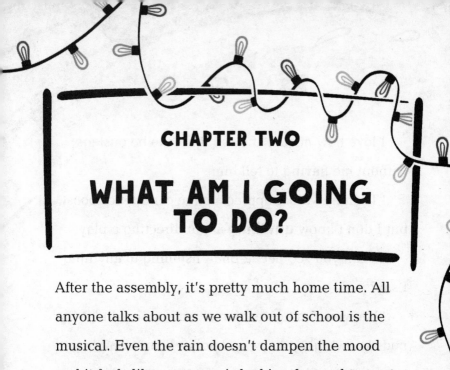

CHAPTER TWO

WHAT AM I GOING TO DO?

After the assembly, it's pretty much home time. All anyone talks about as we walk out of school is the musical. Even the rain doesn't dampen the mood and it feels like everyone is looking forward to next week except me. Milo is over the moon!

"I already know who I want to be," he tells me as we walk home together.

"Really?" I say. "I've got no idea what I'm going to do."

"Don't worry, Neesh, there's a whole list of backstage roles if you want to do something like that. You'd be great as an **assistant director**." Milo smiles encouragingly.

I love how he just knows I'd hate to be onstage, without me having to tell him.

"Thanks, Milo. I appreciate the confidence boost, but I don't know **anything** about directing a play – and can you see Beena Bhatt listening to anything I say?"

"Ha, you don't give yourself enough credit." Milo nods knowingly. "Anyway, laters – I can't wait to get in and start practising for my audition!"

"Wait, you didn't tell me which part you're going to audition for?" I shout after Milo, but he's already run inside his house.

Just then a loud clap of thunder rumbles above me and the rain starts to come down harder. I'll have to run this last bit. I race to my house, but just as I'm nearly there a car drives past, right through a puddle in the road, and soaks me. Great, the perfect end to the day!

I am totally drenched.

Not just a little wet. Not just
a bit damp. I am utterly soaked, head to foot.
I drag myself through the front door.

As I step inside, Granny Jas is about to walk up
the stairs, carrying a pile of towels. "Oh, my goodness,
beta, let's get these wet things off you!" she says,
flinging one of the towels on my head before yanking
my coat off me, making me spin round.

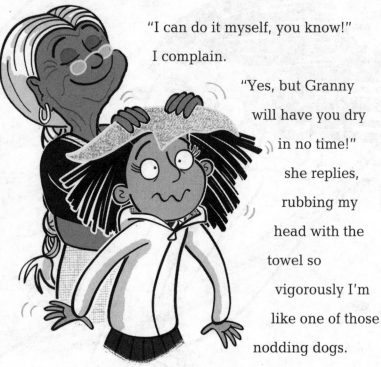

"I can do it myself, you know!" I complain.

"Yes, but Granny will have you dry in no time!" she replies, rubbing my head with the towel so vigorously I'm like one of those nodding dogs.

I can hear thuds and squeals coming from upstairs. "Is Aunty Bindi practising her dance moves up there again?" I ask warily.

Granny chuckles. "No, she's in the loft getting the Diwali* decorations down. You know how she

*Diwali is the five-day Festival of Lights, celebrated by millions of Hindus, Sikhs and Jains across the world. Diwali is a festival of new beginnings and the triumph of good over evil, and light over darkness. Aunty Bindi always puts up way too many lights of course but I kind of like it. When I was little she used to say I was her little helper. I think I made more mess than anything though!

loves to dress the house up at this time of year."

Aunty Bindi's Diwali decorations are legendary. She loves any excuse to put up fairy lights and for Diwali she really goes **all out**. I kind of thought she'd be decorating her own house though, now she's married to Uncle Tony and doesn't actually **live** here any more – although she's always here anyway.

Granny Jas seems to know what I'm thinking. "Yes, beta, I know. She told me she's already done their house, so now she wants to decorate ours too. Apparently, we don't know how to do it properly. Can you imagine, her telling me that I don't know how to celebrate Diwali? Humph. I just leave her to it." Granny gestures as she talks, almost taking my eye out with the corner of the damp towel. "Diwali is not just about all these lights and fancy flower garlands. It's also about the food!" She winks at me. "I made vegetable biriyani for dinner. Go and get changed into some dry clothes and come back down.

I'll make you a warm drink."

I **squelch** up the stairs, trying not to drip too much on the carpet. Uncle Tony is on the landing, holding a ladder propped up against the loft hatch. I can hear Aunty Bindi squealing from inside the loft.

"Sweetums, I found the photo albums!"

Suddenly a box comes **flying** out of the loft hatch at such speed it almost takes Uncle Tony's head off. Luckily, he ducks out of the way and the box of photo albums scatters all over the landing.

Aunty Bindi peers out of the hatch, a string of paper flowers draped around her. "Oops, sorry! I didn't get you, did I? Oh, hi, Anni!"

"Um, aren't you supposed to be getting the Diwali decorations down?" I ask.

"I am! I found the lights and the paper flowers and the clay divas and lanterns with the coloured tissue-paper windows we made when you were little. Remember those?"

"I remember." I smile.

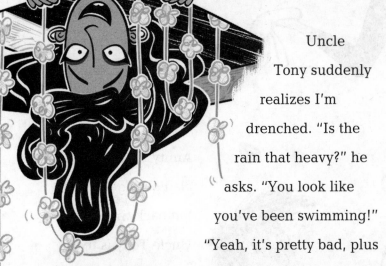

Uncle Tony suddenly realizes I'm drenched. "Is the rain that heavy?" he asks. "You look like you've been swimming!"

"Yeah, it's pretty bad, plus I got splashed by a car," I answer. "I'm just going to get changed."

"Okay, **beta**. Come on, sweetums, we'd better finish up here. We've only got another hour until we have to go and collect the twins from their after-school club and you wanted to check the garage too, didn't you?" Uncle Tony calls up to Aunty Bindi.

"Ooh, one more box," Aunty Bindi pleads. "I've just seen one marked **Fireworks**!"

"Just be careful and *don't* throw it down!" Uncle Tony shouts up **nervously**, as she disappears back into the loft.

I go and change
into my favourite cosy
hoodie and leggings.
When I leave my room,
Aunty Bindi is
clambering out of the
loft backwards and
Uncle Tony is trying
to steady the ladder
unsuccessfully.

"You know, we used to love Diwali as kids," Uncle Tony says. "My brothers and I, we used to act out the battle scene between **Hanuman** and **Ravana**. You know the story of Diwali, right, Anisha?"

"Of course she does!" Aunty Bindi answers for me. "We had that book when you were little, remember, Anni?"

"I remember," I say. "You used to do all the different voices."

"Oh, and I had those little ceramic figures of **Rama** and **Sita** – we used to put on our own little theatre. I must find them. I was very good at the voices, I think!" Aunty Bindi laughs.

We head downstairs where the smell of Granny's fresh puris hangs in the air. Uncle Tony and Aunty Bindi go to the garage to find more Diwali boxes. I go into the kitchen.

"Wash your hands, **beta**, and I'll make you up a plate," Granny says.

I do as she says and then plonk myself on
a kitchen stool.

"So, is there something you
want to tell me about?"
Granny smiles
knowingly.

"Um, no, I don't
think so," I say,
shovelling a big bite
of delicious puri,
biriyani and pickle into
my mouth as fast as I can.

"I'll give you a hint."
Granny makes **jazz hands** at me and grins.

"Are you okay, Granny?" I say, a bit confused.

Granny humphs. "This fell out of your school
bag! Were you just not going to say anything?" She
waves the script at me.

"It's nothing!" I say weakly. "Everyone at school
is dead excited but I'm not even planning to

audition. Acting isn't my thing."

Granny isn't impressed with my answer. "Pah! Not your thing? **Nonsense!** You can do **anything** you set your mind to. And anyway, there are non-acting roles available too – you have to take part but you don't have to perform if you don't want to. It says here that they need people to help behind the scenes as well. It takes a whole team to put on one of these musical productions, **beta**."

I look at Granny with interest. "Since when do you know so much about musicals?"

"I watch those reality shows with Bindi – she loves them." Granny sighs. "Actually, they are not so bad, although always so much drama."

Just then Aunty Bindi and Uncle Tony come in.

"Did I hear my name?" Aunty Bindi asks.

"Anni's school are putting on a musical," Granny blurts out. I cover my ears, ready for the squeal I know is coming – and it does.

"**Annnnnniiiiiiiiii!** That's **AMAZING!**" Aunty Bindi shrieks. "What part are you going for? What play is it? Do you need me to make you a costume? Something with sequins?"

I give Granny a look as if to say, **See what you've done now!** Granny just shrugs and grins at me.

I sigh. "Well, it's a musical about Albert Einstein's life – the script looks interesting, actually. Miss Jive says it shows Einstein was more than a scientist and how important his wife was in his success. I think it'll be good – but before you get carried away with sequins, I'm not auditioning. I can't act to save my life, so I won't need a costume." Aunty Bindi looks horrified so I quickly add, "But I'm going to put myself forward for a support role backstage. It might be fun, I guess." I shrug.

Granny smiles encouragingly. "You'll be great, beta, you have so much to offer."

"I suppose that's still a great way to take part. Hey, if you don't want to act, maybe they need some parents to volunteer?" Bindi says hopefully, looking at Uncle Tony.

"No, I think they have enough people," I reply, perhaps a little too fast. But poor Mindy and Manny would be **horrified** if Aunty Bindi and Uncle Tony got involved in the school play! Super embarrassing! I need to shut this down, quickly.

PARENTS
+
SCHOOL LIFE
=
CRINGE COLLISION!

H_2O ÷ + √

CHAPTER THREE

AUDITION DAY!

The weekend whizzes by in a **whoosh** of Aunty Bindi's Diwali preparations and me mostly trying to duck out of her way. It's soon Monday morning, the day of the auditions, and I'm walking to school. Over the weekend, I studied the script. It's not that long actually and there are only five songs. They are titled:

- **"The Brain is a Sponge!"**
- **"In the Stars" (solo for Mileva – Einstein's wife)**
- **"We Are Sailing"**
- **"E=MC²" (group song with trumpet solo)**
- **"The Power of Dreams"**

The main acting parts are:

- **Narrator**
- **Albert Einstein**
- **Mileva Marić**
- **Paul Drude, scientist**
- **Michele Besso, Einstein's friend**
- **Professor Alfred Kleiner, scientist**
- **Sailor 1**
- **Sailor 2**
- **Einstein's music teacher**
- **Townspeople – for the end song**

I've been thinking a lot about going for the assistant director role. I **have** to put my name down for **something** and at least it's not singing or acting. I might actually be good at it, like Milo said. And I do like Miss Jive, she's a really nice teacher. Even though dance and drama aren't really my thing, she always makes it fun for everyone. All I know is being onstage is **NOT** for me. Something about it just makes me feel so nervous and sick inside. Maybe it's because Milo and I had a bit of a dancing class disaster once? He seems to have forgotten about that though.

Milo is being very **secretive** actually. I still don't know which part he's going to audition for, and he even rang to say he couldn't walk to school with me today. Said he had something to collect from his nan's house first... **Very** odd!

Our whole year group has been told to go straight to the school hall this morning. Outside the hall is a big noticeboard with sheets of paper pinned to it. I find the sheet with all the non-acting roles on it. The roles are listed with blank boxes next to them for us to put down our names if we would like to volunteer for that role.

Director – Miss Jive
Director's Assistant –
Scenery – Manny Singh, Govi Atwal
Lighting – Davinder Kaur

Sound –

Costumes/Props –

Make-up – Layla Bond

Stage help –

Not many people have put their names up yet,
except for Manny and Govi. It looks like most kids
want to be onstage. I can't see Mindy's name.
Maybe she hasn't decided yet. I'm guessing she'll
want to be offstage like me – whenever Aunty Bindi
tries to drag us up to sing along to her **Bollywood**
tunes, Mindy hides behind Uncle Tony, so I can't
imagine she'll want to sing in front of the whole
school.

I pull my pen out of my pocket and write my
name next to **Director's Assistant**. Might as well
listen to Granny Jas and just go for it. There are no
lines to learn, no singing or dancing, it's just helping
Miss Jive – minimal risk, right?

There's lots of pushing as everyone tries to

squeeze in through the double doors of the hall.
Finally, we're all in. I see Mindy, Manny, Govi and
Milo already sitting on the floor in amongst all the
other kids in my class, so I find a space and plonk
myself next to them. "Hey, how did you get here
before me, Milo? I thought you had to pop to your
nan's?"

Milo smiles and taps his
nose. "I **did** go to my nan's
– the thing I collected is
backstage and all will be
revealed shortly!"
We spend the next
ten minutes trying
to figure out
what Milo's
surprise is, with
lots of giggles and silly guesses.

"Is it your actual nan?" Manny asks.

"No, I think it's David Attenborough," Govi says.

"How **cool** would that be?"

"I wish!" Milo says. "I have written to his fan club a few times, though. They sent me a badge and a poster!"

"Let's think logically," I say. "We know it's something to do with the show…"

Milo nods excitedly. "It is, it is! I'm dying to tell you all, but it'll ruin the surprise!"

Milo's saved from saying any more then, because Miss Jive claps her hands together from the front of the hall to signal that we should all listen. "Good morning, children."

We all reply, "Good morning, Miss Jive. Good morning, everyone," in loud unison like we always do.

Miss Jive smiles. "Right, now today is a very special day for Year Six, as you know. It's the audition day for our big production, and we have a number of speaking parts, which is **super** exciting. Now, we already have our school choir and Mr

Notes's music club will be supporting with instruments. The after-school dance club is also going to be taking part – it's shaping up into something **wonderful**!"

Miss Jive holds up a piece of paper from the noticeboard. "Right, I've got the list of volunteers for non-acting parts here, and I can see Anisha Mistry has offered her services as my assistant." She looks up. "Anisha, where are you?"

I duck my head because I wasn't expecting her to call out my name first. Mindy lifts my arm up. "She's here, miss."

"Ah, right, up you come, Anisha. I need all the help I can get!"

I stand up and for some reason everyone starts clapping. My ears and cheeks feel like they're **burning** as I make my way to the front. I wish the ground would swallow me!

Miss Jive hands me a clipboard crammed with about a hundred pieces of paper and starts walking

and talking
at a million
miles an
hour.

"Right,
now we've got
our winning
organizing
team – that's
you and me, Anisha
– shall we begin?
There are some very
important things I want all
of you to remember. Any production must abide by
the rules of the stage. So, I have written up some of
things we must **NEVER** do while working on this
play."

She presses a button on her clicker and the big
screen at the front of the hall comes to life. On it is
a slide that has a bulleted list on it.

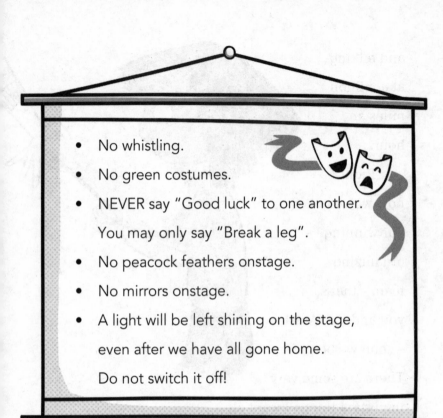

- No whistling.
- No green costumes.
- NEVER say "Good luck" to one another. You may only say "Break a leg".
- No peacock feathers onstage.
- No mirrors onstage.
- A light will be left shining on the stage, even after we have all gone home. Do not switch it off!

There's lots of murmuring in the hall as we read the list. It all seems very odd.

"Um, these rules are a bit **strange**, miss," I say.

Miss Jive turns to me, horrified. "No, Anisha, these rules must be taken seriously. These are long-standing traditions of the theatre. They must be obeyed! We can't afford any **bad luck** to befall our play!"

But then I think she can see how **weirded** out we all are, so she quickly breaks into a smile and continues as if the last few minutes never happened. "Anyway, no time to waste. I want the choir on the left-hand side of the hall, please. Yes, in this corner, that's it. You'll be going to 6A's classroom to rehearse with Mr Notes. Now, can I have any actors who are wanting to audition? I'll have my Einsteins waiting backstage and everyone else here at the front in neat rows, please. Brilliant." She does a quick turn and faces the remaining children. "Anyone who has volunteered for backstage duties, position yourselves in the corner on the right-hand side, please. And that should leave me with the musicians and dancers. Fantastic!" Miss Jive takes a deep breath and then off she goes again. Directing this person that way and that person this way – she's a **whirlwind**!

The backstage helpers go off with Mr Bristles the caretaker to find things they can use as props and to start designing and painting the scenery. Manny and Govi give me a wave as they leave with around ten other kids who have volunteered for the job. Actually, where's Mindy? I didn't get to ask her what she put her name down for.

The dancers start practising their steps at the back of the hall, with one of the dance-club captains leading them. The choir and musicians go off with Mr Notes to a classroom.

That just leaves me, Miss Jive and the actors.

Miss Jive pulls up two chairs for us and calls the first would-be Einstein onstage. For the auditions she's asked the actors not to worry about the script, but to just talk to us in the voice of the character they want to play, the way they imagine them. "**BE** that person!" she told them.

First up is Adil Ansa. Of course **HE** wants to play the lead part! If you haven't met Adil Ansa before,

38

he's a super **brainy** kid in our class. He likes to be the best at everything and he loves the theatre.

Adil bounds onstage, wearing what looks like ladies' glasses and a suit that's clearly too big for him. He's carrying an old-fashioned smoking-pipe and…has he drawn a moustache on his face with felt pen? Oh dear.

I look over at Miss Jive. She doesn't react except for nodding at Adil to start.

Adil stares off into the distance as if thinking deeply. We wait in silence for him to say something, then, just as we think he's forgotten what he was going to say, he raises his hand and shouts far too loudly: "**Two things are infinite: the universe and human stupidity; and I'm not sure about the universe.**"

Miss Jive goes a little **pink**. "Hmm, I admire your knowledge of Einstein's words but I'm not sure that's what we're looking for, Adil."

Adil frowns. "I'm getting into character, miss.

Einstein was a **complex** man – it's not easy being a genius!"

Miss Jive clears her throat. "Okay, well, do you have more to show us?"

Adil nods and stares off into the distance again. He raises his hand to his eye and wipes away an imaginary tear. Then he places his right hand on his chest and starts to speak very slowly, each word taking ages, with at least a ten-second pause between each one. The whole time he gestures with his pipe in hand, pointing meaningfully at the audience – well, me, the other actors and Miss Jive. "The important thing is not to stop questioning. Curiosity has its own reason for existence. One cannot help but be in awe when he contemplates the mysteries of eternity, of life, of—"

Miss Jive interrupts him. "Okay, well, I think we get it, Adil. That's wonderful. We should let others have a try now, though. Only fair."

Adil looks annoyed at being cut off mid-speech but comes off the stage and plops himself next to us. "I need to be able to watch my competitors," he reasons.

So we watch another would-be Einstein, this time a girl from one of the other Year Six classes, Yasmeen. She decides to mime her audition very meaningfully, using her hands to demonstrate that she's staring up at the universe and then looking in a microscope and then pretending to write on a board. The whole time she's making strange expressions which leads to some giggles from the rest of the group watching. Then it's the turn of a boy called Tyrone, who is painfully nervous and completely forgets what he wants to say. This is not going well at all. Each Einstein we see is a bit worse than the last and it's starting to look like we might have to let Adil do it after all.

Then Miss Jive calls out, "Can we have the next person auditioning as Einstein, please? I believe this is the last person we're seeing for this role." Adil looks delighted at this news. He's obviously thinking that if this one is as bad as the others, then the part is his for sure.

There's a cough and a strangled sound from behind the curtain onstage.

"My name is Albert Einstein," the voice says.

Wait, I recognize that voice!

And then he comes out – it's **Milo**! But not as we know him.

Milo looks **amazing** – he actually looks like Albert Einstein! He's wearing a grey messy wig, a false grey moustache and even fake bushy eyebrows! He's got a brown sweater on, with a white collared shirt under it and grey tweed trousers. The biggest surprise, though, is what he's carrying. A cat! He places the cat down on the floor next to him and does a bow down to her, like you would to a royal person. Then the most surprising thing ever happens – the cat bows her head and holds her paw up for Milo to hold.

Milo smiles and then stands up to continue, still fully in character. "I am a scientist. You may know me for my theories and my discoveries, but did you know I was an animal-lover too? Meet Tiger, my pet cat."

Miss Jive smiles. Milo is doing so well. Next to me, Adil huffs loudly, but all the other actors waiting to audition just ignore him and carry on listening to Milo.

"Did you know my name, Albert Einstein, is an **anagram** of Ten Elite Brains? That's because I'm so brainy! Although I have a really bad memory, so I often forget simple things like my own phone number!"

That makes everyone chuckle. Milo then finishes up his audition with a song called "We Are Sailing", which is in the script for the musical. According to the song, Einstein was a keen but not very good sailor – he used to get lost a lot!

Miss Jive stands up to applaud, and everyone

else joins in too. Milo was
brilliant and hilarious!

"The cat is a touch
of genius, Milo!"
Miss Jive
congratulates him.

"This is my
nan's rescue cat,
Molly." Milo
points gleefully to
the cat. "I've
trained her myself
– she can do all sorts
of things."

"That's wonderful,
Milo. You did really, really
well!" Miss Jive beams.

Milo jumps up and punches the air in celebration.
Molly the cat looks pleased too – as pleased as a cat
can look, anyway.

When everything has settled down again, it's time for the auditions for the leading lady, Mileva. First, Beena Bhatt struts out, wearing what looks like a fake-fur coat. Two of her besties stand either side of her, primping her hair and spraying hairspray at her. She swats them away. I shake my head. Only Beena Bhatt would have an **entourage** for a school play audition.

Milo stands at the side of the hall, looking quite **scared**. If he does win the lead role, being married to Beena would probably make it a lot less fun!

Miss Jive gives her a thumbs up. "Okay, show us what you've got, Beena. Good luck!"

Beena smiles sweetly and starts. "I'm Mileva, Einstein's wife. He adores me, but I think he spends too much time with his stupid experiments."

Miss Jive **splutters** as she's sipping her cup of tea and sprays it everywhere. "Beena, dear, that's not the sort of thing she'd say, is it? There's lots of great material you could have used for **inspiration** in the script – what about the scene where she's helping him with his equations? Mileva was very supportive of Einstein. Have you read the scene at the kitchen table?"

Beena rolls her eyes. "No, but *I* think she would be annoyed that he paid so much attention to his work. And you said we have to act how we think they'd act. This is my interpretation of the role!"

Miss Jive frowns. "Yes... Well, that's not exactly what I meant. Have you got a song you can show us?"

Beena **sighs**, annoyed. "Well, yes, okay. I didn't like any of the songs in the script, so I created my own number. I would use it in the play if I were you. Anyway – Layla, Amani, get out here!" she hisses to her friends.

They totter out from behind the stage curtain, grinning nervously.

Beena starts her audition again, this time with

her entourage. They do a weirdly aggressive song about being the best, but they are so out of tune, I have to cover my ears, which makes Beena give me a hard stare. They finish with Beena in the centre doing a star-shaped pose and shaking her hair wildly.

Miss Jive clears her throat. "Um, I think we've seen enough, Beena. Is there anyone else back there who wants to audition for this role?"

Silence.

"Oh, I thought we had Mindy going for this one. Maybe she changed her mind?" Miss Jive says.

Mindy? I think to myself. *I've never even heard her sing. And why wouldn't she have told us she was thinking of auditioning?*

A minute later Mindy is onstage, looking like she wants to be sick. The hall goes quiet.

"I hope she's okay, she's looking a bit peaky," Miss Jive says to me.

"I'm sure she'll be fine, she's probably just nervous," I say, willing Mindy to do well in my head.

Mindy clears her throat a few times, yanks her cardigan sleeves over her hands and folds her arms around herself. I've never seen her this **uncomfortable**. She's usually so sure of herself.

Miss Jive shouts out some encouragement.

"Mindy, just do your best, there's no pressure. I know you can do this."

Mindy forces a smile. "Okay, I'll try."

I give her a thumbs up and mouth, *"You've got this."*

Mindy closes her eyes and takes a deep breath. Her arms fall to her sides and she starts to sing. Everyone stops fidgeting and just listens.

Mindy sings a song about being a girl and having so many dreams. I recognize it from the script – it's called "**In the Stars**" and it's beautiful.

The way Mindy sings it is so emotional and meaningful – I had no idea she could sing like that! Miss Jive has tears in her eyes and at the end she stands up to clap loudly. I stand up too and clap with her. I'm so proud of Mindy. Everyone else in the hall joins in as well.

Miss Jive says, "Well done, Mindy!"

Mindy just looks shocked and overwhelmed.

Beena quietly **seethes** in the corner and then stomps away while we're all still applauding. She doesn't deal well with not being the centre of attention.

Milo goes over to Mindy, beaming. "I hope you get the part, Mindy! I **DO NOT** want to be married to Beena if I get the part of Einstein!"

"**Ha**, you don't know what kind of wife I might be yet!" Mindy raises an eyebrow at him. "And you do know Einstein's wife was just as smart as him, don't you? He would never have become famous if it wasn't for her," she tells him knowingly.

Milo shrugs. "That's okay, I like smart girls, that's why I'm friends with Anisha."

Mindy groans and laughs. "You're too nice, Milo. I can't be mean to you now."

I touch Mindy's arm. "I never knew you could sing like that. You always hide when Uncle Tony puts the karaoke on."

Mindy smiles sadly. "My mum – you know she left us and went away to be an actress in **Bollywood**? Well, I guess I get my voice from her. I don't like to sing in front of Dad, though. I guess I think it might make him feel weird. But I do love singing and when this play came up, I thought I might…you know, just see if I'm any good. Miss Jive was really encouraging when I told her I might audition."

"Any good? You're **amazing**!" I say. "And I reckon Uncle Tony will be so proud of you."

Mindy beams. "Do you think so?"

"Yes, and you know Bindi will be all over this. She's going to want to manage your career." I laugh.

Mindy covers her eyes. "Oh no, you're right! Is it too late to back out?"

Milo chuckles. "Um, yes, I think so – plus you can't leave me now. If you don't take the part and Beena gets it, my life won't be worth living!"

MILO

+

BEENA

=

DOUBLE DRAMA DISASTER!

After that the auditions go by quite quickly, thankfully without too much trouble. The whole time, Molly the cat sits quietly under my chair, preening herself. There's only one odd moment, when Maryam from the other class auditions to be one of the sailors. She's standing in our makeshift boat onstage when she says she feels seasick!

"But you're not actually at sea!" Miss Jive points out.

"No, but I believe I am at sea and it's making me feel all whirly," says Maryam, her eyes wide and a hand to her mouth.

"Maybe you'd be better with a land-based role then," Miss Jive says kindly.

Later, Miss Jive asks me what I think of each actor and makes notes on her script. I realize I'm enjoying myself – it's quite fun being involved in the decision-making, although I told Miss Jive I'd rather not pick between my friends for the lead parts.

Maybe being **part** of the school musical will be really **exciting** after all?

CHAPTER FOUR

DECISION TIME!

After break, Miss Jive tells everyone to quieten down as she's about to make the big **announcement** of who has which part.

"Now let me say first that everyone who auditioned did tremendously well – it's not an easy thing to get up here and act in front of everyone. So I'm super proud of you all." Miss Jive beams. "But there can only be one Einstein and I think we all saw that there was one particular actor who shone onstage. So, without further ado, our Einstein is going to be…Milo!"

There's enormous cheering then. Milo stands up and takes a bow, holding Molly the cat. I can see

Adil in the corner sulking.

Miss Jive moves on to announce who will be Mileva. "I think this person surprised us all, but she is very deserving of the part and will be brilliant. Everyone, let's give Mindy a round of applause!"

Mindy looks at me – she's shocked that she got it.

I lean over and tell her, "You did it! Well done!"

Everyone claps – except Beena, obviously.

Mindy says, "I can't believe it, Miss Jive really thinks I'm good enough!"

"Well, I can," says Milo, stroking Molly.

Manny joins in. "Me too. You think I don't hear

you singing into your hairbrush in your room sometimes? I think you could be in the running for winning the drama-academy place – you're that good, sis!"

Mindy blushes and looks down at the floor. "Oh, I don't know. I really want to make the school proud, but I've never performed in front of an audience before. I don't think I can seriously win the place."

I nudge her. "Yeah, but what if you do?"

Mindy grins. "It **would** be the best thing ever! And you really think Dad will be proud of me?"

"**SO** proud!" I say.

Miss Jive goes on to cast the parts of the other scientists, sailors and villagers. There are cheers and claps when each part is announced. There's some disappointment for those who didn't get the parts they auditioned for, especially Adil and Beena, but even they soon get caught up in the excitement of the production.

Finally, it's time for some proper rehearsals to

begin. As Milo and Mindy and the other actors get ready, I go and find Govi and Manny with the kids who are painting scenery with Mr Bristles backstage. They're making the most beautiful and vibrant park scene, complete with flowers and trees, as well as a backdrop for the inside of Einstein's kitchen, which has cupboards and a sink painted on it. I'm so impressed!

Then I walk round to the classroom where the choir and musicians are practising. They sound a bit **screechy**! And now Beena has joined them with her trumpet! She said if she couldn't be the leading lady then we didn't deserve to see her acting **magnificence** anyway and her trumpet solo was going to be a **show-stealer**. To be honest, her trumpet-playing isn't much better than her acting... I don't say that to her, though!

Meanwhile the sailors practise a sea shanty from the script – they're quite good – but the scientists are still trying to make sense of their lines.

"So is it '**E equals MC two**', like the number?" Noreen, the first scientist, asks.

"No, duh, it's obviously '**E equals mac two**'," Ade, the other scientist, replies. *It's a good job they're only pretending to be scientists!* I think to myself, as I explain to them that it's actually "**E equals MC squared** – only Einstein's most famous equation!"

The dancers continue practising their routines at the back of the hall with their dance captain giving

them instructions and Miss Jive moves between them and the stage, trying to supervise both. The dancers have misplaced their music, so they have to hum the tune for now, but they're all humming at different speeds. Then they have to pair up and there's a bit where they have to twirl each other. Not everyone remembers to turn on time and then someone goes left instead of right. I try counting them in to help. Eek! I hope they get the hang of it soon.

"Jacob, this way – like I showed you. And arms up, not down!" Miss Jive sighs, demonstrating what she means.

Meanwhile, the costumes are being hung up on a rail in the dressing room backstage. There's a group of kids matching up accessories and putting the outfits together. There's even a special front-of-house team made up of Jess and Amelia. They're designing a poster for the play on Miss Jive's iPad and putting together a programme – it looks awesome already.

It's all starting to feel like a **real** musical.

I do my best to help wherever I can. I take notes for Miss Jive, move things around onstage and help remind people of where they should be in the script. I feel useful, and I start to get quite excited about this play as I see it come to life. It's like we're all one big team trying to achieve something huge – and I think we might actually do it!

Finally, Miss Jive and I sit back down to watch Milo and Mindy rehearse their first scene. One of the girls from our class, Tara, is the narrator.

She starts dramatically. "Let's go back in time,

way back to 1902, when a young couple are working by candlelight on a very special maths problem."

Milo smiles cheesily. "My dearest wife—" he begins, but Mindy stops him mid-sentence. She puts her hand up, looking **horrified**.

"Milo Moon, have you taken your socks off?"

Milo grins, clearly pleased someone has noticed. "It's well documented that Einstein liked to walk around barefoot. I'm just getting into character like Miss Jive said we should."

Mindy frowns. "I think you're taking it too far, Milo. This might have to be a short marriage!"

Milo folds his arms defiantly. "Well, I'm not sure I like being married **anyway**!"

Mindy copies his folded arms. "Fine by me!"

Miss Jive jumps up. "Now, children, remember it is just acting. It's supposed to be fun! Milo, I have to sort of agree with Mindy. Perhaps you should pop your socks back on – it is a bit chilly, after all," she says diplomatically.

Right on cue, Molly strolls over with Milo's socks in her mouth.

"Aww, Molly, you're such a good kitty. If you want me to put them back on then I will," Milo says cheerfully.

Miss Jive sits back down.

"Thank goodness for Molly!" I say.

"Oh yes, definitely!" chuckles Miss Jive.

The rest of the afternoon goes really **well**, and the fact we only have a week to get this show ready doesn't seem **quite** so worrying any more.

"Thanks for all your help today, Anisha." Miss Jive smiles as we tidy up the last couple of chairs at the end of the day.

"I didn't expect to enjoy myself, but I did," I admit.

"Well, go and have a nice restful evening – we need all your energy this week. Tomorrow we have a delivery of stage lights coming. We don't have any budget to buy some, so another school is lending us some of theirs."

"Oh, that's kind of them," I say.

"Hmm, it is – but I wish we didn't need their help, if I'm honest," Miss Jive says.

I wait for her to say more on the subject, but she doesn't.

"Okay, miss. I'll see you tomorrow then."

"Night, Anisha."

I leave with Milo, who is holding Molly in her carrier and chats non-stop about the play as we walk across the playground and out onto the street. We're almost at the end of the road when I realize I've left my clipboard in the hall. It's got my copy of the script with all my notes of what we're doing on it. I wanted to have a look over it this evening, to prepare for tomorrow's scenes.

"Shall I come back with you, Neesh?" Milo offers.

"No, it's fine, I'll only be a minute. You carry on, Milo," I say.

Milo shakes his head. "And have your Granny Jas tell me off for leaving you to walk home alone? No way. I'll wait here with Molly, thank you."

I laugh. "Okay, okay, you're right. Back in a sec then."

I run back to school – it's starting to rain again – and race into the main building and down the corridor to the hall.

Miss Jive seems to have left and the hall is empty. I spot my clipboard on the edge of the stage and grab it. I'm just about to leave when I hear hushed voices coming from the corridor. I don't know why, but instead of just walking out of the hall, I crouch beside the stage and listen. Something about the tone of the voices sounds shifty.

"This play is going to be a **disaster**!" one chuckles – a young voice, I think.

"Shhh, someone could hear you," the other voice scolds. This one sounds like a grown-up – a man.

"There's no one around!" the younger voice says.

"And you said she's always having a **disaster**, so it's sure to become true. What was that name you said you used to call her? **Jittery Jive?**"

"Ha, yes, but don't let anyone hear you say that! Anyway, be that as it may, we need to act as if we support her," the older voice reasons. "You **can** act, can't you?"

"Ha, yes, sir, I can!" the younger voice answers. Then I hear them walk away.

My cheeks burn hot again. I feel angry for Miss Jive. She's such a kind, caring teacher and she really wants our school to do well. How **dare** these horrible people say Miss Jive is a disaster! I can't believe anyone from our school would be so **mean**. I just wish I knew who it was. I just don't recognize their voices. In any case, I decide there and then that I'm going to do whatever I can to make sure this show is a huge success – we'll show them who can do a good job!

CHAPTER FIVE

SOMETHING STINKS (NOT MILO'S FEET!)

Today is Tuesday. We've got just four days left to rehearse and prepare everything for the show on Friday afternoon. I'm looking forward to getting back into school and starting work. We're going to make this play brilliant.

The hall is buzzing with excitement when Milo and I walk in. The dancers are already practising their moves at the back and there's a cacophony of musical instruments being tuned up onstage, with Beena being the loudest, of course. Poor Mr Notes is trying to take charge, but Beena just barges in front of him, waving her trumpet around! Milo puts Molly in her carrier down near the stage. She seems unbothered by all the noise, thankfully.

Miss Jive smiles wearily as I walk up to her. "Morning, Anisha. I think everyone's got stuck in already. Before we do anything else, let's go and get the scenery boards the boys started to make yesterday. They're in the dressing room at the back."

I ask Govi and Manny to come along to help and we all head backstage.

"We've had so many lovely donations of props too. I'm excited to show you." Miss Jive beams as she pushes the door open.

OH NO!

The room is a disaster! There's a big crack in the ceiling above the two scenery boards that Govi and Manny were painting yesterday and water dripping from above. There's a shallow pool of water on the floor and the paint on the scenery has all run and it's just a giant soggy mess!

We all just stand there, taking in the scene of destruction in front of us. Mr Bristles comes up

behind us and stands in the doorway. "Oh, my giddy aunt, what happened here?!" he says.

"Our scenery has been **destroyed**!" Govi exclaims.

"I was so pleased with how we'd done it as well. Gutted," adds Manny.

Miss Jive wrings her hands in despair. "It looks like there's been a **leak** and the roof gave way. We will have to start all over again! This is a day's work lost, not to mention the cost of the materials and the fact we only have a few days left to get everything ready."

"I've been telling Mr Graft we need to do something about the roof! I'll get a mop and call the builders. Always a drama in this school," grumbles Mr Bristles.

"We'll help clean up!" I say, nodding at my friends.

"Of course we will!" Manny says. "I'll go and ask Milo and Mindy to take a break from rehearsal and come too."

Miss Jive smiles at me gratefully as Manny rushes back to the hall. "Thank you, everyone. Honestly, what are the chances of something like this happening?"

I touch Miss Jive's arm. "Don't worry, we can fix this. Look, it's mainly the park scene that's damaged. I'm sure Manny and Govi could do something with it once it's dried out. Let's move the boards to the other dressing room. It's warmer and less soggy in there."

"Yeah, miss, me and Manny won't give up yet!"

Miss Jive wipes her eyes. "You are an excellent assistant, Anisha, that's a brilliant idea. I'll go and make sure the radiator is on in there. You could make a start on getting the boards out but stay away from the crack." She leaves the room just as Manny returns with Milo and Mindy.

"Woah, what happened?" Milo asks.

"Looks like a leak," I reply. "Right, let's try and move the scenery out. Just be careful where you tread."

I step cautiously into the room, putting my clipboard down in a dry spot on a table, my feet making a **splat** sound in the shallow puddles.

I look up at the crack again. Something's

bugging me about it, but I don't know what. I look around at the floor. Then I realize.

"Look at the ceiling, you two. Notice anything weird?" I ask.

"Um, not really – apart from the big crack in it," Milo answers. "Maybe they'll replace those ceiling tiles now. They were a bit stained and yucky."

"The tiles! **Exactly**, Milo! Notice anything odd about them?" I prompt.

Mindy catches on to what I'm getting at. "The tiles, of course!"

Milo is still clueless. "Huh?"

I point to a pile of tiles on the floor – the polystyrene kind that schools and offices sometimes have on their ceilings. You'd expect that when the roof leaked, the ceiling tiles would have fallen and cracked and ended up lying around on the floor. But they're not. Instead, there is a neat pile of faded tiles, enough to cover the crack in the ceiling.

"It almost looks like someone pulled those down,

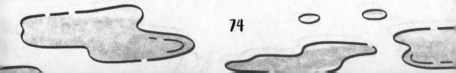

deliberately made a bit of
a crack in the roof above,
maybe with a pole or
something, then let the
rainstorm do its damage,"
I say.

"Do you really think
so? That seems like a lot of effort," Milo says.

"It just seems a bit suspicious, Milo. My gut is
telling me something is wrong here," I say.

"Well, you're usually right about these things,
Neesh. What do we do?"

"For now I think we just need to move the
scenery boards like Miss Jive asked. Hopefully it
was just a one-off prank or someone being a bit
mean."

That's when I remember the conversation I
overheard yesterday.

"Milo, when I ran back into school to get my
clipboard last night, I overheard two people talking.

Someone was saying they didn't think Miss Jive was going to do a good job on the play. I thought it was just people being **nasty** – but what if they took it further and decided to **mess up** our scenery?"

"That's awful if it's true," Mindy says, looking anxious. She doesn't say it, but I know Mindy is thinking of her dream to go to the drama academy – anything that could ruin the play could ruin her chance of winning the place too.

"Don't worry, Mindy. I could be wrong," I say, trying to reassure her.

"Come on, let's get the scenery boards out of here. I'm sure we can fix them up a bit," Manny adds. Govi steps forward to help too.

As they move the first board, which is thankfully on wheels, I have to watch where I step on the wet floor as I shuffle around it – and it's then that I notice something. Next to where I'm standing is a large, damp, muddy footprint!

"Am I seeing things or does that footprint look way too big to belong to Miss Jive?" I ask, pointing at it.

"Woah, that's at least a size eleven, I reckon!" Mindy marvels.

"How do you know that?" Milo asks.

"My dad has big feet, probably about that size, and he's an eleven," Mindy replies.

"Okay, well assuming your dad hasn't been in here, Mr Bristles didn't even step inside when he saw what happened so then who else would have been in this room?" Milo asks.

"That's what we need to find out!" I say. "Something really stinks in here."

"Well, it's not my feet, before you start," Milo replies.

"No, something stinks about what's happened here in this room," I explain.

"But it would be great if you could **PLEASE** put some socks and shoes on, Milo," Mindy mutters.

"Alright, but I want it noted that you're stifling my creative growth," Milo replies stubbornly.

"Milo, Mindy, can we **concentrate**, please?" I say. "So, we agree something weird is going on. If someone did deliberately damage the scenery then they might try to mess with the rest of the play. At the very least we should be on the lookout for anything **suspicious**. Agreed?"

"Ooh, do we get to investigate, Neesh?" Milo asks excitedly. "Mindy and I can be undercover. You know, cos we're in the play."

Mindy shrugs. "That's not the **worst** idea you've ever had, Milo. We might spot something from up onstage. If someone is messing with the play, then we'll see it."

I nod. "Okay, let's get the damaged scenery moved to the dressing room and then you two go back to the hall. We'll catch up later at my house after school and you can tell us if you've seen anything suspicious."

We move the boards, the others go back to the hall with Miss Jive but I trail behind. Miss Jive turns. "Are you coming, Anisha? Mr Bristles is coming to tidy up, so let's head to the hall and try and get our morning started."

I think quickly. "Coming, miss! I'll be there in a sec."

Milo and Mindy look at me curiously but walk out with Miss Jive. I look again at the footprint. I didn't notice before, but it has a **zigzag** pattern to it. The shoe it came from must have a zigzag pattern on the sole! I grab my clipboard from the table and pull off a piece of blank paper. I place it down carefully on the wet muddy footprint. I lift the paper up and it now has an exact copy of the footprint on it. It might not be any help...but it could be a **clue** to helping us find out who is messing with our scenery!

DAMAGED SCENERY
+
ZIGZAG FOOTPRINT
=
TIME TO INVESTIGATE!

CHAPTER SIX

MUSICAL MAYHEM

My head is swimming. Could there be a **saboteur***
among us?

I look around the hall. Mr Notes is already
onstage with the musicians and the choir now,
ready to help them rehearse.

"Right, let's have a go at the very first bit when
the curtain opens, shall we? That first note is so
important, it sets the tone for the whole
performance," Miss Jive says. "Can someone pull
the rope to release the curtain so it closes, please,
and we'll practise?"

One of the backstage helpers unwinds the rope

* Someone who deliberately tries to destroy something = saboteur!

from its holder on the wall and lets it go. The two curtains swing from their open positions to meet in the middle of the stage. But, wait, that's not right... A **HUGE** hole has been cut out in the centre of one of the curtains! Miss Jive and the choir peer through it from their side of the stage.

"Umm, that's not meant to be there, is it?" Beena asks. Even she seems a bit **shocked**.

Miss Jive has turned a little pink in the face. "Well, no, Beena, it is not, there should be a lot more curtain! This can't be a good sign. Maybe the **moths** got to it?" She rubs her forehead, looking worried. "Let's open the curtains back up. I'll see what we can do about that hole, and in the meantime everybody remind yourselves of the rules of the theatre, please. I'm sure I heard someone saying **'good luck'** earlier and we really can't have that kind of thing, okay, because look what happens! I had the rules printed on the backs of the scripts. This just won't do, it really won't."

She walks off, muttering about needing to check her horoscope and remembering to put her script under her pillow tonight – apparently that's another theatre superstition. I'm not sure it's going to help though. This is starting to feel more and more like sabotage. I look around the hall. Who in here would want to stop the production?

But then everyone is so excited to be part of this. Plus, that footprint looked too big to belong to anyone in our year. And that hole in the stage curtain was **huge** – it would take an awfully big moth to eat through that much fabric...or a lot of effort from a person to **cut** through the material.

Could it be a grown-up? I guess I have to consider everyone. I start a list on my clipboard.

Okay, so, **first**, there are the people I overheard. I write that down. And the muddy footprint could have belonged to one of them – but it could have belonged to someone else, so I add that too.

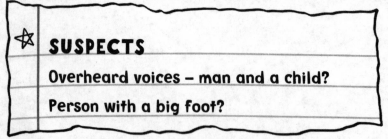

✩ SUSPECTS

Overheard voices – man and a child?

Person with a big foot?

I sigh. It's not a great start. Before I can think about it any more, Miss Jive is back in her seat and the musicians start to play. First up is Jeremiah on keyboard. He plays three notes, one after the other, again and again. Then Anya on the drums starts tapping a light beat. Then Ola on the guitar strums a tune. They sound okay at the moment – maybe they've got their timing together now? Miss Jive smiles encouragingly at them. "**Keep it up!**"

Just at that moment, an **awful** noise comes from the right of the stage and out walks Beena Bhatt, blowing enthusiastically on her trumpet. She sounds like an **elephant**! I put my fingers in my ears. Jeremiah puts one hand over one ear and continues to play with the other. Anya does the same. Beena looks like she's enjoying herself though.

Just as I think it can't get any worse, a screeching emerges from the left side of the stage. It's worse than the noise a piece of chalk makes scraping against a chalkboard. Who on **earth** is making that awful sound? Is it the cat?

I look around, but Molly is sitting still under a chair, licking her paws. She's such a good cat, so well behaved. Beena responds to the **screeching** sound by blowing even harder into her trumpet. Miss Jive stands up to stop everything, but then **Milo** comes out onstage. That **awful** noise is coming from him! Well, from the violin he's attempting to play.

Beena stops trumpeting and stomps over furiously. "**WHAT** are you doing?"

"I read that Einstein played violin," Milo says, grinning. "I thought it would be a nice addition to the musical."

Beena **snorts**. "It might – if you could actually play it, Milo! And besides, I'm the one doing a solo in this piece, not you. Isn't it enough that you got the lead part and now you want the **spotlight** here, too?"

Miss Jive interrupts. "Okay, let's calm down. That's a lovely idea, Milo, and I applaud you doing extra research on your character. However,

I'm not sure it's quite right for this song – but maybe you could do a little bit during one of your later scenes?"

I quickly add in, "Mr Notes might be able to show you how to play a couple of basic notes, right, Mr Notes?"

Mr Notes looks **sceptical** but nods. "We can try."

Milo seems happy with that and Beena is back to being the loudest musician, so she's happy too. **Phew**! Crisis avoided!

Just when I think things have settled down, Miss Jive gasps, "Oh no, **NO**, **NO**! We can't have this!"

"What is it, miss?" I ask, worried.

Miss Jive points to one of the dancers, who has just walked into the hall.

"Sorry I'm late, miss, I had the dentist this morning. My mum did phone the office," she says.

Miss Jive doesn't uncover her eyes and just says, "Lara, I need you to remove that...**that** thing!"

Lara looks just as confused as the rest of us.

"What thing, miss?" she asks, looking down at herself.

"That **scrunchie**," Miss Jive mutters.

I look at the increasingly baffled Lara. She has long hair tied in a side ponytail with a bright green velvet scrunchie.

"Green, Lara. It's **green**!" I shout. "Remember, **no green allowed** – stage rules!"

Lara finally understands and quickly whips out her scrunchie.

"It's gone, miss!" I say brightly.

89

Miss Jive breathes a sigh of relief. "Oh, thank you, Anisha. Please, children, try to remember: stage rules are very **important**! We've already had a minor **disaster** with the scenery and another with the curtain; we don't need any more bad luck!"

Everyone settles back into what they were doing and Mindy comes over to sit with me while Miss Jive busies about the stage, adjusting the props and moving people around.

"Wow, that was intense!" Mindy says.

"Yeah, Miss Jive really believes all that stuff."

"You don't, though?" Mindy asks.

"No, I think there's a logical explanation for most things. Including what happened to that scenery and the curtain," I say.

"I really hope it was just an accident. I wasn't sure about taking part in the play to start with and I know we've only rehearsed a little bit, but I really love it, Anisha," Mindy admits. "And the chance to go to stage school even just for the summer would be amazing. I talked to my dad last night and told him how much I love singing. You were right, I shouldn't have worried, he was so supportive!"

"Aw, I'm so glad." I say, "Shall we look the academy up online? I've never seen it."

So we find the Dreams Dance and Drama Academy website on Miss Jive's tablet. Mindy points out all the great facilities they have, like a recording studio and vocal coaches, and her whole face **lights up** as she talks about it. I've never seen her look so happy.

While Mindy happily scrolls through the website, I start thinking about the damaged scenery again. I play the conversation I overheard yesterday evening back in my head.

That voice – the older one – who could it have been? A teacher? Clearly someone who doesn't think Miss Jive is the right person to be in charge of the show…

My eyes wander to the set of doors at the other end of the hall and that's when I see him. Mr Fields the PE teacher. Why is **he** in here? We've got the hall booked for rehearsals for the whole week, so all the PE lessons are outside. It seems **odd** for him to be hanging around like that. He's scribbling something on paper too and grinning. He looks up and sees me staring at him, frowns and leaves through the doors. Very **suspicious** behaviour!

Could it be Mr Fields sabotaging the show? But why would he want to stop the play? And does he have big feet? I didn't get a look at them.

I write his name down on my list. He's got to be worth **investigating** – I at least need to get a closer look at his shoes. I think about following him right away, but then Miss Jive calls me over to help her pull up the slide with all the theatre rules on it again. I put an exclamation mark next to Mr Fields's name on my list and set my clipboard down on my chair. I just hope nothing else goes wrong before I have a chance to **solve** this mystery.

CHAPTER SEVEN

SPRAY-PAINT SABOTAGE!

It's 11 a.m. now and Miss Jive sends the musicians and the choir off to the music room to practise some more. Beena trumpets her way annoyingly **loudly** all the way down the corridor so we can still hear her. The actors who have been rehearsing in one of the classrooms come onstage and start running through some of their lines. I'm watching Mindy and Milo rehearsing a scene where they get married. Milo is really getting into character now, which is making Mindy **scowl** a lot.

"Milo, you're not listening! Miss Jive said not to do it like that!" she complains.

"You know, Einstein didn't respond well to authority. He was far too clever to be told what to do," Milo says knowingly. He's starting to sound like Adil Ansa, never mind Einstein!

Mindy is not impressed. She grits her teeth for the tenth time today. "Milo, I can't deal with this right now, I just can't! Let's try it again properly, or I swear I'm quitting and Beena can have the leading lady's part!"

Milo looks panicked. "**NO!** I mean, you know, of course we can try it again."

I chuckle to myself. Who would ever have thought Milo and Mindy would be acting in a play as husband and wife?

Mr Fields, who is loitering at the back again, smiles over at Miss Jive and she goes to talk to him. Maybe she'll tell him to go away or ask why he's being a lurker! But she doesn't do either of these things. Instead, she looks like she's telling him something – she puts her hand to her head and then waves her arms about and points up at the ceiling like she's describing something. He looks confused and then upset. Then, even weirder, they both come over to me!

"Anisha, Mr Fields is going to give us a hand backstage with some of the scenery and props. We need lots of extra **help** if we're going to have this play ready by Friday with the setbacks we've had."

Mr Fields flashes his teeth at me. "Reporting for duty!" he says, and salutes me. "Miss Jive told me about the scenery," he explains. "It's an **awful** thing to happen, so I'd like to help if I can."

I nod, still **suspicious** of him. I try to check out his feet, but I can't tell if they're the same size as the footprint from the dressing room. So I smile and make my excuses to go to the loo. I need a moment to make sense of all this.

Miss Jive and Mr Fields get pulled into practising with the dancers and as I leave I see them both trying to copy that move some kids do called "the woah". They're getting their arms all in a knot though.

I leave the hall and head to the girls' toilets. It's quiet in there, thankfully. I go into a cubicle and I'm just about to sit down when someone else comes into the toilets. Well, two somebodies, to be precise. And they're whispering!

I can't help but listen. I realize there's a gap in the cubicle door where the lock has been replaced a bit lower down. I peer through the hole. It's two girls from the year below us.

"Did you get the can of gold paint?" one of them says to the other.

"Yeah, we can sneak in at lunchtime and finish it off."

"Great – we have to make sure no one sees us though."

"Okay, but will it work?"

"Of course it will! If we do this, it will fix that scenery for good!"

They giggle and then I hear them leaving. I can't believe it! Did I just hear them plotting to ruin the play scenery for good? But why? Whatever the reason, I have to **stop** them.

My mind is racing as I wash my hands and leave to go back to the hall. They said they were going to finish it off at lunchtime, which is in half an hour. I quickly make a plan in my mind. I'm going to catch them in the act. **No way** am I letting them get away with this!

When Miss Jive sends everyone off for lunch, I tell Milo I'll be there in a second and hang back and hide behind one of the big curtains onstage – making sure it's the one without a hole in it! It's a bit dusty back here, but luckily I don't have to wait long before I hear the girls from the toilets coming into the hall.

"The scenery boards are backstage – I heard one of the boys from Year Six telling his friend," one of them says.

"Okay, but we have to be **quick**," the other one replies.

"Why? We've got a whole hour before lessons start again!"

"Er...yeah, but I want some lunch as well. I'm starving and there's pizza on the menu today."

"Alright, let's just get on with it. This is going to be **SOOOOO** good!"

They climb up on the stage and for a second I think they're sure to realize I'm hiding behind the curtain, but they don't. Phew. They open the backstage door and go through it.

I have to follow them – I
can't let any more **damage**
happen. I poke my head round
the door first to make sure
they aren't still in the
hallway. Then I walk down
the corridor and listen at the
dressing-room door.
They're in there – I can
hear giggling. What do I
do now? Should I just
jump in and confront
them? Maybe I should
go and get Miss Jive? But
they might leave and I need
to catch them in the act!

I push the door open but when I do I accidentally
knock the clothing rail with all the costumes for the
play on to the floor in a **big heap**. I step inside to try
and pick the rail up but don't notice the can of paint

on the floor next to me and I put my foot **right** in it!
Oh no, gold splodgy foot, paint scattered
everywhere. But where are those two girls?

"Hello?" I call out.

"**Mmmmmpfh**," comes a reply from somewhere
within the pile of clothes. I pull away a pair of
trousers and a big frilly dress to reveal the very
dishevelled-looking girls. I hold out my hands to
help them both up. They're both covered in gold
paint too.

"Sorry I knocked you over but what are you both
doing in here?" I ask sternly. "Were you going to
destroy the scenery boards?"

They look shocked. "**NO!** We would never!
It was supposed to be a surprise for Miss Jive!"

"What was?"

They both start talking over each other then and
pointing frantically to the scenery boards, which are
facing away from us.

"We did this abstract art project a few weeks ago. When we heard about what happened to the scenery we wanted to help. Well, it was Ava's idea. I'm Ayesha, by the way," one of them says.

"Help how?" I ask, suspicious.

"By using the technique we used in art to make a colourful backdrop for the play. We thought a spacey/time-themed backdrop would be cool. So we found some old boards from last year's nativity and painted them. We came in early this morning and we just wanted to finish up then surprise Miss Jive later! Look! What do you think? Einstein was into space and time, right?" They turn the scenery boards around to face me. They're right – it *does* look like stars in the night sky. I have to admit, they've done a good job.

"So you were going to…"

"…try and help," Ava finishes. "We were just finishing up with the gold flecks and then you startled us and we got covered in the gold paint!

WAIT! You thought we were trying to destroy them? Do you think someone damaged them on purpose in the first place?"

I eye up Ava's small feet and Ayesha's too. Definitely not big enough to be a match to the muddy footprint. I weigh up in my mind how much I should tell them.

"Well, I'm not sure at the moment. I'm just watching out for the play and helping to make sure it goes ahead smoothly," I say. "That's the job of the director's assistant, right?" I smile. "I should get back to the hall and do just that. You guys had better hurry and get some lunch."

Ava smiles back uncertainly. "Oh okay, we will."

Just then the door opens behind me and it's Miss

Jive along with Manny and Govi.

"Oh my goodness, what happened here?" Miss Jive exclaims.

"Woah," says Govi. "Did you make that scenery? It's **awesome**!"

"Cool!" agrees Manny.

"Ava and Ayesha wanted to help," I explain.

Miss Jive squeals, "They are **amazing**, thank you so much, girls. What a wonderful surprise! We were just coming back here to get some props and other bits."

"We've made a bit of a mess," Ava admits pointing at the paint on the floor and on herself.

"Hmm, yes, I see that. Well, we can clear that up, I think it's a washable paint. Of course, it might have been better if you'd worn aprons!" Miss Jive jokes.

We all help them pick the costumes up off the floor and then Ava and Ayesha go off to get cleaned up. Govi says he needs to go to the library, so Manny and I set off to find the others at lunch. I can't help feeling a bit disappointed that I didn't catch the culprit after all. But then I remind myself it's never the first or even the second person you suspect. I **cringe** as I remember the time I thought my own Granny Jas was a suspect when Uncle Tony went **missing** right before his wedding to Aunty Bindi.

In the dining hall we find Milo and Mindy stuffing their faces with pizza.

"Everything okay, Neesh?" Milo asks.

"Well, sort of," I say. I tell them about everything that just happened with Ava and Ayesha.

"So, if it's not the Year Fives who caused the damage to the scenery, then who?" Mindy asks.

"Well, I had an idea before the whole thing happened with Ava and Ayesha," I say. "Have any of you noticed that Mr Fields has been lurking around the hall the past day or so?"

"The PE teacher?" Manny says. "Why would he be interested in our play?"

"Well, I'm not entirely sure," I admit. "He was just **hanging** around at the back of the hall at first, scribbling something in his notebook, and then when Miss Jive told him about the damage to the scenery he acted surprised and said he wanted to help. But I just can't shake the feeling that something about him is **off**," I reply.

"Maybe **HE** wanted to be in the play and he's angry that he's too old?" Manny suggests.

I can't help but smile. "I don't think it's that, Manny. But maybe he wanted to run the show himself? Or maybe he just doesn't like Miss Jive for some reason."

"Maybe he just doesn't like musicals?" Milo adds. "Although I can't see why not. Musicals are awesome!"

I nod. "Remember the conversation I **overheard** last night in the corridor? What if that was him saying how he thinks Miss Jive won't be able to handle the play? He could just be pretending to be nice to her face. And I bet he has big feet!"

"The footprint!" Mindy exclaims excitedly. "Do you think it could be a match?"

"I don't know for sure," I admit, "but if I could just get close enough, we might be able to tell."

"There's no way to do that without looking suspicious." Mindy sighs.

"Hmm, there might be," I say. "He teaches PE so maybe he keeps a pair of trainers in his office for lessons. We just need to get in there to look!"

"Ooh, a secret **stealth mission** to retrieve evidence," Milo whispers, looking around.

"We'd have to find a way to get out of rehearsals when we know Mr Fields won't be in his room – and we'll have to be quick," I say.

We head back to the hall after lunch and I realize straight away there's someone I don't recognize here. I don't think he even works at our school. He's wearing a long navy-blue coat with very unusual shiny brass buttons that look like theatre masks and he has a smart suit on underneath. He strides over to Miss Jive by the stage and hugs her! She doesn't really hug him back though, so it's a bit **awkward**. I wonder who he is? I try to get a bit nearer.

I hear him saying, "Oh, darling, I came over to deliver that lighting you need and to wish you luck, but then our old friend Miss File in the school office just told me what happened."

He seems familiar, but I don't think I've met him before...

Miss Jive frowns at him. "We're fine, honestly."

The man smiles. "You don't have to put on a brave face for me, darling. You must be devastated! I hear all the scenery was totally ruined."

"Ah, well, actually we're all sorted I think. Some

of our students have already made new scenery. I've got a very resourceful team, Bill," Miss Jive replies curtly. I get the feeling she doesn't like this man very much.

I decide to go and interrupt. "Miss Jive, I just wanted to check something… Oh sorry…you're busy talking," I say.

Miss Jive looks glad of the interruption. "Ah, Anisha, this is an old colleague of mine, Mr Script. His school is lending us some lighting for the play. Anisha is assisting me," she says to him. "I'm **surprised** you had time to come over here, Bill, haven't you got your own production happening too? Mr Script teaches at a school across the other side of the city," she explains.

Mr Script beams at me. "Anisha, that's a **lovely** name. Well, yes, we are also hoping to catch the attention of the drama-academy scout. Actually, I know your school is a first timer in the competition but I know the academy well – we've won the summer-school programme places quite a few years in a row now. But I'm always thinking about how I can share my talent and experience with others and I want you to know I'm here for you." He **almost** seems genuine but I'm still not sure about him.

Just then Molly the cat shows up and starts purring and weaving her body in and out of his legs.

"She likes you, I think," Miss Jive comments.

"I've always been **good** with animals." Mr Script chuckles, bending down to stroke her.

I guess he must be alright. Cats don't normally trust just any one. That's what Milo told me anyway.

CHAPTER EIGHT

GROSS!

The next day is Wednesday. Time is running out and we still aren't any closer to working out who might be trying to sabotage the play. Luckily there haven't been any more **disasters** yet but I just **know** the crack in the ceiling and the hole in the stage curtain were not accidents. I'm a bit nervous about what might happen next! Milo, Mindy, Manny and I meet up in the playground to discuss what we're going to do.

"Are you sure about this, Neesh?" Milo asks. "I mean, I like Mr Fields, he's a cool teacher – I can't imagine he'd want to ruin the play."

"Yeah, and he really didn't look like he knew

anything about the scenery or the curtain yesterday. Actually, I heard him offering to help move some chairs," Manny points out.

I think for a second. He might be right, **only**...

"What if he only wants us to **think** he doesn't know anything? I saw it in a movie once. But he doesn't know that we know he knows something!" I say triumphantly.

"Yeah, but, Neesh, what if **WE** don't know that he doesn't know that we know that he knows something? What about that?" Milo asks.

Mindy frowns. "Huh?"

I shrug. "Look, all I know is that Mr Fields has been **lurking** round the hall when he has nothing to do with the play and I still don't know if it was his voice I overheard on Monday. That's **got** to be worth investigating. If we don't find anything, we'll move on to looking at other suspects. Deal?"

Everyone reluctantly agrees to the plan. Milo and

I will sneak out of rehearsals at some point this morning and go to Mr Fields's office. Hopefully he'll have a spare pair of shoes in there and I can match the size of one of them to the print I took from the dressing room. Simple, straightforward, should be **no problem**.

Rehearsals start off okay and about an hour into the morning Mr Fields comes and says he needs Miss Jive to come and check something with him. This is my chance. I signal to Milo: **WE NEED TO GO**.

We wait a couple of minutes and then make our way out of the hall and down the corridor to Mr Fields's office. Everyone else in the school is in lessons so it's super quiet. We tiptoe and wait outside his door. I can't hear anything.

"Okay, Milo," I whisper. "I'll push the door open, we'll creep in, find the shoes, check if the print matches, then leave. Mr Fields could come back at any minute, so we need to be quick."

Milo nods. "Silent but deadly!" he whispers and puts a finger to his lips.

We push the door open and walk straight in.

To our **surprise**, Mr Fields is there! Even **more** of a surprise, Miss Jive is there too, reading what looks like the piece of paper Mr Fields was scribbling on yesterday! Miss Jive jumps when she sees us and throws the piece of paper to the side, but it lands face up on the floor near us. I lean down to see. It looks like a love letter! There's a big kiss and a love heart at the bottom. That doesn't make sense. Then I look up and realize...

The love note isn't the worst thing. They're doing something totally gross.

Totally unexpected.

They're **HOLDING HANDS**!

"Um…oh, Anisha, was there something you needed help with?" Mr Fields blushes, stumbling over his words.

"Anisha, you really should knock before entering a room!" Miss Jive says, also turning a deep shade of **pink** and immediately letting go of Mr Fields's hand.

Milo and I say nothing, still **shocked** at what we've just seen.

Mr Fields chuckles nervously. "I see we've taken you by surprise. I suppose it doesn't hurt for you to know…Miss Jive and I are…um –" he scratches his head – "**dating**!"

Milo and I look at each other, totally cringing.

"Um, that's nice," I say, starting to back away. "We'd better get back to the hall, sorry for barging in."

"Hang on, Anisha!" Miss Jive calls out.

"You obviously came in here for something. What was it?" Mr Fields asks.

I look at his feet. "Ah, nothing, it can wait," I say and we back out of there **FAST**.

Once we're out in the corridor, Milo and I just stare at each other. "What was that?" I say.

"I know! Kind of gross for teachers to be all **lovey-dovey**! But then…you know, I think it's quite sweet," Milo says. "Miss Jive looks happy."

"That's true," I say. "But it doesn't help us figure anything out. If Mr Fields is Miss Jive's boyfriend, then he's probably not the one **sabotaging** the play. And I can't check his shoe against the footprint now anyway."

Milo grins. "This might help with that!" and he pulls one of Mr Fields's shoes out from behind his back.

"How?" I ask, baffled.

"When you were talking, I spotted his spare pair just by the door, so I quickly grabbed one while they were busy being embarrassed."

"Amazing!" I marvel. I pull the muddy footprint from my clipboard and hold the shoe up to it. It doesn't match **at all**. No zigzag pattern on the sole.

"It's about two sizes too small as well," Milo says.

"That definitely rules him out then," I say. "Now what?"

Before we can think further, there's a **SCREAM** from the direction of the hall. It's so loud that Mr Fields and Miss Jive come out of the office behind us. "What's going on?" they both ask.

There's **another** scream and we all start running to the hall. When we burst in it's chaos, and it takes me a second to realize what's actually happened. The stage is a mess. A chair has been kicked over and the curtain hanging nearest to it is covered in shiny liquid. Weirdest of all, Molly the normally well-behaved cat is miaowing loudly and rolling around wildly on the table that we've been using for the kitchen scene. There's more spilled liquid and what looks like glitter **EVERYWHERE**!

Miss Jive gasps. "What on earth?! Milo, what is wrong with your cat?"

"I don't know, miss," Milo cries. "I'll get her – maybe she's ill."

We run up to the stage while Miss Jive and Mr Fields calm everyone down. Molly is behaving very strangely. She's knocked over pretty much everything that was on the table – a bowl, a load of glitter tubes and some glue, which is the shiny liquid that's gone all over the floor, curtain and table. I don't know why any of that stuff was on the table in the first place. It doesn't make sense!

Milo grabs Molly and tries to calm her down.

"MOLLY, WHY?!" Milo says, **disappointed**.

Molly looks up and I know cats are usually not

bothered by much, but I swear she looks so **guilty**!

CHAPTER NINE

BOSS BEENA AND BINDI'S BLACKOUT!

There's so much **mess** everywhere that the stage is unusable. The glue is sticky and the glitter is making the actors sneeze. It's a big **gloopy** disaster. Miss Jive tells us all to go to the big classroom, 6C, which doesn't feel so big once we're all in there. She goes off to find Mr Bristles to start cleaning up the hall and asks me to keep rehearsals going as best we can.

But with all the pandemonium, everyone seems a bit unnerved. I check in on the choir in 6A, which is the connecting classroom next to ours, and it's **not** going well. They keep **forgetting** their words and Mr Notes has to keep asking them to begin again.

I think he's starting to **panic** that there isn't enough time for them to get everything right. The musicians are no better and Beena's solution still seems to be to play louder than everyone else, which, of course, sounds **awful**. Back in 6C, the room is in chaos as the actors and dancers are all trying to rehearse at the same time too. Molly sits in her carrier in the corner, sulking – she seems to have calmed down at least! I wonder what got **into** her?

Milo and Mindy come running over.

"Anisha, we need your help. We need to get everyone focused and working together."

I look around at the noisy room. "How? I'm not trying to be negative, but this lot are never going to listen to me. We need someone they'll follow."

Wait a minute, I know who that is. But oh, I wish it wasn't!

"I know who can help us get everyone's attention," I say.

Mindy studies my face. "No. It's not who I think it is...is it?"

"I'm afraid so. I'll go and get her." I sigh.

"She'll be impossible after this, you know. Us asking **HER** for help!" Mindy warns.

"I know but she is the **loudest** one here," I reply.

I open up the connecting door to the classroom with the choir in and then head over to the musicians, who are all practising at once and not in time – as usual. Mr Notes seems to have popped out for a second.

"Beena, can I talk to you?" I ask. She's so busy blowing into her trumpet that she doesn't hear me straight away.

"**BEENA!**" I shout, just as everyone stops playing at the same time so it's basically just **me** shouting.

"No need to shout!" Beena says. "What do you want?"

"Can I talk to you for a sec?" I ask, really wishing the ground would swallow me up.

"**YOU** want to talk to **ME**?" Beena asks. "Okaaaay…"

"Look, this play is coming apart. We were doing okay, but after the damage to the scenery and Molly's meltdown just now, everyone seems to have lost their focus – surely even you can see that? We need everyone's attention to get them working together. And I thought **YOU** might be able to help us with that."

"And what if I don't want to help you?"

"Beena, think about it. If we don't get everyone organized, this play is going to fail, we don't win the trophy and no one gets a place at the drama academy.

I know you don't like to lose."

Beena thinks for a second. "Well, losing is for losers, obviously, and I'm no loser! Alright, I'll help. But **YOU OWE ME**," she says, and I know I'm going to regret asking her. But it's for the play.

Beena takes a drink from her water bottle, stands up on her chair and lifts her trumpet to her mouth. "You might want to cover your ears," she tells me. Then she blows as hard and as long as she can. It's so **LOUD**!

It works! Everyone stops bickering, yelling, singing, dancing and playing their instruments.

The kids in the next classroom turn to look, all eyes on Beena. She smiles, loving being the **centre of attention**, of course. "Listen up, you lot. We need to get organized. This play is a **shambles**! We'll never get that trophy or that drama-academy place at this rate. Get with it, people! **FOCUS!**"

"So, what's your solution, Beena?" someone shouts from the back.

"Well, as much as I **dislike** working with others, I have decided it's our only option." Beena says, totally taking credit for what I said to her a few minutes ago. She carries on. "Anisha here will co-ordinate and you **WILL** listen to her, got it?"

There's a reluctant murmur of agreement from a few people – and that's it. Beena gets down from her chair and says to me, "You're welcome," like she's suddenly **solved** everything.

I take a deep breath. "Okay, let's start with you musicians: you're not playing in time," I say. Beena frowns but I continue. "You all need to listen to Anya on the drums. If you all keep time with her, it'll sound much better! Try it!"

Beena huffs. "Mr Notes said that too but I just thought he was being annoying. Alright, Anya, you start and we'll join in."

I smile and turn away.

I work my way round the two rooms, giving tips and advice. I always thought my observation skills were just useful for **mystery solving** but they come in handy here too! I tell the dancers to space out a bit, so they stop **bumping** into one another. The number they're working on involves a complicated move where they stand in a single line facing the audience and then they take turns to circle their arms to the side creating a wave effect. They just can't seem to get it right! I count them in to get the timing perfect so that they all move together at the right moment. We just have to hope they can do it on the night.

I remind some of the actors about making eye

contact and looking more natural when they're moving around. Most of it is common sense but it seems to work. Soon everyone is working as a team – giving each other space and supporting one another, instead of trying to be the centre of attention.

"**Wow**, Anisha, you did it!" Milo says as I approach him and Mindy, mid-rehearsal. "I knew you could."

"Yeah, well let's see how long it lasts!" I say.

Miss Jive comes back then. "Everything is looking very organized in here, Anisha, well done!"

"I had some help," I admit.

Miss Jive smiles but then spots someone getting a mirror out of their bag and rushes over to stop them. She really is serious about this superstitious stuff! "First that green scrunchie yesterday, now this! No wonder we're having so much bad luck!" she mutters.

As everyone is getting on okay now, I decide to

see if I can help clean up in the hall with Mr Bristles and our school cleaner Mrs Bucket. I'm just scraping some of the hardened glue carefully off the stage with a plastic spatula when I spot something completely out of place. It's small and green, looks a bit like a grape but it isn't, and it's half covered in glitter. I know exactly what it is because my Aunty Bindi loves them. It's an **olive**!

I look around on the floor and there's **another** one – and **another**. I lift the bottom of the stage curtain and find there's a load here that were probably kicked under when Molly was rolling around all over the place. Why would there be olives here though? They aren't part of the props for any of the scenes. I put one of the glittery olives in my pocket. It might be evidence. I'm not sure what it's evidence of yet, but something tells me it could be important.

Later on, Milo, Mindy, Manny and I all walk home together. The twins are having their tea at our house today so we can spend some time coming up with a plan. Our investigation into Mr Fields didn't exactly work out but I guess we **eliminated** a suspect, so now we need to figure out who else it might be. And the way Molly **freaked out** seemingly over nothing is bugging me too.

"So, do we still think someone is messing with the play?" Milo asks.

"Yes, definitely," I reply. "The damage to the scenery and the curtain was almost certainly set up and there's something about the way Molly was behaving that was so strange and out of character."

"Molly's such a good cat normally," Milo agrees. Then he looks horrified. "She's not on your suspect list, is she?"

"Right now, Milo, **EVERYONE** is a suspect, so we need to be on the lookout," I say.

"What? Even us? I'm just painting scenery!" Manny complains. "It feels a bit unfair to suspect me. I haven't done anything."

"Not us, you doofus!" Mindy scolds him. "Obviously none of us have a reason to want to stop the play. Well, maybe me, so I don't have to be married to **barefoot badly-violin-playing Milo**!" She giggles.

"Hey, the violin-playing wasn't that bad, was it?"

Milo protests. We all start laughing and then run the rest of the way home, with Milo **chasing** us and shouting, "I'll play it some more! You watch! I will and I'll get better! Then you'll see!"

We're out of breath when we get to my house and the smell of Granny's scrumptious cooking is wafting into the street. Aunty Bindi is halfway up a tall ladder outside the house attaching lights for Diwali.

Uncle Tony is standing at the bottom of the ladder, looking very worried.

"**Sweetums**, maybe I should be up there and you hold the ladder?" he asks.

"No, I need to do it, honeykins. I want it to look amazing and I saw this woman on the internet putting her lights up in a very specific way," Aunty Bindi replies.

We shout hello and leave them to it.

"Are you sure it's okay for me to come for tea as well, Neesh?" Milo asks as we go in through the front door.

"Don't be silly, Milo, you know you're part of the family. Granny loves you especially, because you appreciate her food so much. Maybe just pop Molly in her carrier here in the hallway for now though. I'm not sure Granny will want Molly running round the kitchen."

Right on cue, Granny comes into the hallway where we're taking off our shoes. "Ah, there you are, **bete**! I hope you're all hungry. I've made far too much food as usual. I was trying out some new Diwali recipes, so there's going to be lots to eat in about an hour."

"Granny, you're the best," I say, hugging her.

"Can we help?" asks Mindy.

"Well, you know I don't like anyone messing about in my kitchen, but I'll make an exception for you four. Wash your hands and you can help me make some **roti**. And leave that cat there in the hallway."

I smile at Milo knowingly.

We follow Granny into the kitchen and take turns to wash our hands.

Granny gets her big steel bowl out from the cupboard and puts some chapati flour in it. She adds boiling water and then carefully mixes and eventually kneads it into a dough once the water has cooled. She gets Mindy to separate the big ball of dough into smaller separate balls. Milo is then given a board and a really thin rolling pin called a velan. Granny shows him how to make a circular pancake – a roti. Milo's aren't really circles, but Granny tells him not to worry. Manny has a go too, and his come out like lopsided rectangles.

"So, how is your big play coming along?" Granny asks us as she cooks a roti on her tawa.*

"Well, there might not be a play if things keep going wrong," I say.

Granny puts her hands on the counter. "Why? Tell me, what happened."

So, we do. As we tell Granny everything, she nods and frowns and shakes her head. "Sounds very suspicious! And I bet the teachers have no idea who is behind it."

"They think it was just a couple of unfortunate accidents," I say.

Granny waves her rolling pin at us. "Pah! Well, you'll figure it out, **beta**! If anyone can, it's you!"

"Yeah, exactly!" Mindy agrees.

Just then Aunty Bindi comes in from the cold. "Right, Mistry family, are you ready for a lights extravaganza?"

* A tava or tawa is a flat frying pan. Also known as a tawah, thawah or thavah, the pan is round and is usually around twenty to thirty centimentres wide. But in professional kitchens they can be up to a metre wide! Imagine a roti that big!

With a bit of **grumbling** and **groaning**, everyone puts their hats and coats back on and heads outside. We stand facing our house. There are quite a few wires trailing from all over the front of the house, leading to a weatherproof plastic plug box.

"Are you sure this is all safe, Bindi?" Dad asks.

Aunty Bindi waves him away. "Yes, I know what I'm doing! Now are you ready?"

"Ready," we all say in unison.

"Three, two, one…lights on!" Bindi flicks a switch on the remote control she has in her hand, but nothing happens. So she presses it again. Still **nothing**. "Hmm, I thought I plugged it all in properly," she mutters to herself, following the wires. "Ah, look this connection is loose," she says, finding two wires that have round plastic connectors on the end. She pushes them together. Suddenly the lights on our house come on in a blinding flash, but then there's a big bang and everything goes dark.

Not just our house either – the lights in every house on our street go out! People come out of their front doors to see what's happened as Dad checks we're all okay. Oh no, here comes Mr Bogof, our annoying neighbour from down the road, charging towards us like an angry bull!

"Is it **YOU** that's caused this power outage,

then? I might have known it would be. With your garlands and your lights – it's totally unnecessary if you ask me," he booms.

"Well, we didn't ask for your opinion," Dad says, going a little pink in the face. "And we'd kindly ask you to keep your opinion to yourself."

Mr Bogof grunts and huffs a bit more but doesn't say anything else.

"I'll go and call the power company and see if there's anything they can do at their end," Dad says.

Aunty Bindi sniffs. "I just don't get it. We had the same number of lights up last year and it was fine."

Granny Jas humphs. "My food is going to be ruined. I told you we need a gas cooker, but no, you wanted that fancy electric one and now look! Dinner is only half-cooked!" And she goes inside, complaining loudly.

Aunty Bindi looks sheepish. "Anyone for sandwiches?"

CHAPTER TEN

MOLLY GOES FLOOPY!

Once we're inside, Granny Jas continues complaining and pointing at the half-cooked food. Dad is on the phone to the electric company and Mum fiddles around with the fuse box under the stairs. Uncle Tony finds some candles and goes round placing and lighting them so we can see where we're going. Molly is miaowing loudly, so Milo takes her out of her carrier and we all sit in the living room.

"Well, this is an interesting way to spend the evening," Mindy remarks.

"Yeah, not what I was planning," I agree.

Aunty Bindi comes in holding a cookbook triumphantly. "I knew leaving this book here would come in handy."

"Is it a guide to electricity?" Manny asks.

"No, silly, it's a cookbook." Aunty Bindi grins.

"How can we cook with no electricity? And even if it comes back on you know what happened last time," Mindy says carefully.

"What happened?" I ask, remembering my own baking **disasters** with Aunty Bindi when she lived here.

"Nothing happened, just a slight **misjudgement** on the difference between a tablespoon and a teaspoon," Aunty Bindi insists. "Come on, you four, you can help. Granny Jas is sulking because she thinks dinner's ruined, but I think we can save it with this book and a few key ingredients from the fridge."

I look at the others sceptically, but we all follow her into the kitchen. Molly slinks alongside Milo obediently. She's back to her normal **well-trained** self again, thankfully!

"What kind of food can we make without the cooker?" I ask.

Aunty Bindi proudly shows me the front of her book. "No-cooking recipes!"

"Humph!" Granny Jas grunts from the other side of the kitchen. "What is this?"

"It's all recipes we don't need the cooker for! Look at this one – it just needs salad, bread, cheese, tomatoes and olives. **Yummy**!" Bindi answers. "It'll keep us going till the power comes back on. I think I have a bag of nice tortilla chips in the cupboard too and salsa! I like to leave some of my favourite treats here for when I visit and fancy a snack."

"Ooh, we can have a picnic," Manny says.

"I guess a picnic could be fun and there's some still-warm roti and pickle as well." Granny Jas grins, coming round to the idea.

"Yum! I'll have a bit of everything," says Milo, kneeling down and stroking Molly, who is still quite **sparkly** from all that glitter as she lies stretched out on the floor. She closes her eyes and starts to doze off.

"I think all the mayhem earlier has worn her out!" I say.

While Molly snoozes, we all pitch in and help. Manny washes the salad then Aunty Bindi chops it up, Mindy and I arrange everything on the plates, Milo grabs the cutlery and Granny Jas gets out all her favourite chutneys and pickles and places them next to the big pile of roti we made earlier.

We're just getting ready to sit down when Molly, who was being so calm, suddenly jumps up on the counter.

"Get down, Molly!" Milo scolds.

But Molly does not listen. Instead, she starts sniffing the bowl of olives.

"I didn't know cats like olives. Paws off, kitty!" Aunty Bindi wags her finger at Molly, who pays no attention and continues trying to get the olives out of the bowl. She puts her paw in and pushes down, tipping the bowl up and sending the olives **everywhere**.

Then she starts rolling around in the olives and miaowing! Milo tries to reach out for her but she wriggles free.

"Um, what is she doing?" Mindy asks.

"It is very **strange**," I say, a thought forming in my mind. "Just like the way she was behaving at school."

"What happened at school, Anni?" Aunty Bindi asks, as she tries to shoo Molly away and protect the other bowls of food. "You know what, let me just move all this to the other counter," she says, and she starts transferring the food to the other side of the kitchen.

I decide to say my thought out loud. "Milo, remember when Molly went **bonkers** on the stage and knocked the glitter all over the place and started rolling around in it?"

"Yeah, she just got scared probably. Or it was an accident," Milo replies, trying to wrestle Molly back into her carrier. "Molly, what is wrong with you?

Have you forgotten all our training?" he pleads.

"What if... what if Molly knocked that glitter over because she had the same reaction she had just now?" I say.

"To what? Olives? They don't do anything, do they?" Milo asks.

"Let's look it up," I say.

Mindy pulls out her phone and searches **Cat reactions to olives** and a whole load of information comes up. "Wow – it looks like olives have the same chemical compound as **catnip**!" she announces.

"What's **catnip**?" Manny asks.

"It's a herb that cats **love** – it makes them roll

about and smush their face into wherever it is. But it says here olives have the same effect," Mindy replies.

"But there were no olives at school," Milo points out.

"Um, I think there might have been," I say. "**Look!**" And I go to my jacket pocket and pull out the glitter-covered olive I found on the stage floor earlier.

"Okay, hang on, what are you saying here, Neesh?" Milo asks. "Someone's **framing** my nan's cat? Because you know she wouldn't mess things up on purpose! Would you, Molly?" He lifts up her carrier to his face. Molly is showing her bottom through the little window though.

"I think you might be right, Milo. Molly didn't knock over the glitter or the glue on purpose – she couldn't help it. But what if someone wanted to ruin our play, found out we have a cat on set and wanted the cat to cause some **chaos**? Molly is so well-behaved that the only way they could make her go a little floopy is to put some catnip in front of her.

Maybe they thought that would be a bit obvious and then they found out about olives!"

"There's a lot of ifs and maybes there, Anisha," Mindy says.

"I know," I admit. "But it's too much of a **coincidence** to ignore. I think someone deliberately put olives on that table and knew it would have that effect. Why else were they there when they aren't on the props list or part of any scene? There's no other **logical** reason."

"Okay, so what do we do? We've got no way of knowing who put them there," Milo points out.

"True – but it is another clue, and we can't give up our investigations now. There's too much at stake," I say. "The school's reputation, the play, Mindy's dream of going to the drama academy. I'm not going to let someone **ruin** all that," I say, **determined**.

"We're with you, Anisha." Mindy smiles.

"And me!" Manny exclaims.

"And me too!" Milo grins.

Suddenly the lights come back on.

"Ah, the power company must have sorted it," Bindi says. "I knew I hadn't broken the electricity really!"

Just then Mum pops her head round the kitchen door. "Bindi," she whispers, "we need to go."

"Go where?" I ask.

"Just got to pop out, **beta**, back later!" Mum grins. "Bindi, come on!"

Aunty Bindi looks excited and squeals. "Coming! You children carry on and eat. We'll eat when we come back."

Granny Jas pops her head out from the fridge. "Oh yes, I need to go too."

"Where?" I ask. "Aren't you going to finish your cooking?"

Mum answers, "**Dentist**," while Granny replies, "**Shop**," at exactly the same time.

Granny grins. "You know, shopping for new

teeth. I'll finish the food later, you have all those snacks, you'll be fine." And they all disappear before I can ask any other questions.

"They're up to **something**," Manny remarks.

"Do you think so?" Mindy asks. "I mean, Bindi's **always** that excited. Granny was being a bit sus, I suppose."

"Definitely," Manny agrees.

I laugh. "I think we'd better concentrate on

one mystery at a time. Now let's eat first, I'm **starving**!"

Manny and Milo want to eat in front of the telly, so Mindy and I sit in the kitchen with our plates for a bit of quiet.

"I haven't asked you how rehearsals are going in the middle of all this," I say.

Mindy takes a drink of water before answering. "Okay, I guess. I really love singing and I love being part of the show, but if I tell you something, promise not to say anything to anyone?"

"Of course," I say.

"I'm a bit **scared**," Mindy admits. "The big solo is such a huge responsibility and what if my voice isn't up to it?"

"You sang a bit of it for the audition, didn't you?"

"Yeah, but I didn't have to hit the high note at the end for that short piece. I can do it in my bedroom at home. I'm just scared I won't be able to on the night in front of all those people!"

"I'm not good at being in the **spotlight**, Mindy, so I'm probably not the best person to offer advice, but I know this – you were **born** to perform. You've just got to grab the opportunity with both hands."

Mindy smiles. "Thanks, Anisha. I'm going to try my best."

Later on, we're enjoying some of Granny's home-made popcorn and trying to come up with a plan, when Mum, Dad and Granny come in from the car, carrying two big boxes and a bag.

Manny jumps up. "Here, Uncle, I'll help," he says to Dad.

Dad flinches. "Um no, that's okay, **beta**, we've got it. Just got to put these in the shed."

Mum makes a funny high-pitched sound and says, "Yes, we…er…must get these put away. You carry on doing whatever you're doing, children." And they all back away towards the garden.

Quickly.

Mindy, Milo, Manny and I all look at each other.

Grown-ups can be so weird and secretive sometimes!

CHAPTER ELEVEN

THE VOICES!

The next day is Thursday. How is it Thursday **already**?

Last night, I hardly slept, tossing and turning. When I did sleep, I dreamed that Milo, Mindy, Manny and I were running after Molly, who was chasing floating olives and clipboards, while Beena's trumpet blared at us all. I woke up **exhausted** and no nearer to understanding anything that's happened. Whatever today brings, the show **must** go on. The play is tomorrow! I'm still excited to be part of the play but I can't wait to get to the weekend and celebrate Diwali with everyone and **relax** a bit!

The twins get dropped off at my house early so we can all walk to school together.

"So, what's the plan, Neesh?" Milo asks, as he joins us from his house.

"I'm not sure yet. I'm hoping there will be some more **clues** left behind onstage at school that we might have missed. I also think we need to tell Mr Graft and Miss Jive what's going on now too. Normally I wouldn't involve the grown-ups yet, but we can't risk the play being cancelled or sabotaged on the day – so we need their help."

"Yeah, and we'd better rehearse too. If we're going to save the play from being ruined, then we need to know our lines. We still haven't got that scene right," Milo says to Mindy.

"**Ugh**, the one where we get married?" Mindy moans. "I don't see why we need that one. Mileva's marriage didn't define her. She was a strong, bright woman in her own right. If anything, Einstein just slowed her down."

"Hey, that's a bit rude," Milo complains, coming to an abrupt halt in the middle of the pavement.

"Well, it's true," Mindy replies. "Mileva should have her own play, really."

"Let's keep walking and talking," I suggest, sensing Mindy has a lot she wants to say on this topic.

After much discussion and Mindy giving us lots of examples from history where men took credit for female achievements and Milo surrendering the argument because he knew he couldn't win it, we arrive at school. We're deliberately early, because I need to find Mr Graft before school starts. As it happens, he's already in the school hall with Miss Jive.

"Ah, children, you're early," he comments as we walk in.

"We have something to tell you, sir," I say.

Mr Graft raises his eyebrow at us. "Okay, is this a **good-news** or a **bad-news** situation?"

"Bad, I'm afraid," I say. "Someone is trying to sabotage the play." I take a deep breath and let my words hang in the air for a second.

Mr Graft looks at Miss Jive and she looks back at him, confused.

"I know we've had some mishaps and bad fortune, Anisha, but I'm not sure it's **sabotage**. If only everyone would stick to the rules of the theatre, we might be okay!" she says.

"We've got **proof**," I say.

"What proof?" Mr Graft asks.

"Well, for starters, when the scenery was damaged, the ceiling tiles looked like they'd been pulled down deliberately and placed neatly to one side," I say. "Not to mention the big hole that had clearly been cut out of the stage curtain! And then yesterday when Molly went loopy and knocked the glitter and glue everywhere, that wasn't her fault. There was a bowl of olives on the table. We found out that cats react to olives like it's catnip!" I realize when I've finished that my proof doesn't sound like much – but I'm sure I'm right.

Mr Graft frowns. "Look, Anisha, I admire your determination and you have been right about these things in the past, **BUT** I have to agree with Miss

Jive. I don't think this is a case of **sabotage**. Tiles, olives...it's not enough to convince me, I'm afraid. Now, we have a show to put on so let's concentrate on that, yes?"

I sense there's no point trying to argue. We need more proof before the grown-ups are going to listen. I nod and head back over to Milo, Mindy and Manny.

"Is that it?" Mindy asks.

"For now," I whisper. "We need more proof."

"They never listen to us," Milo complains. "And we're almost always right!"

"They want proof, we'll get them proof," Mindy says quietly. "This is my one chance to do something that's really **important** to me and someone is trying to **ruin** it. We know it and everyone else needs to know it too."

Just then there's a **commotion** outside the hall, so we all go to see what's going on, including Mr Graft and Miss Jive. It's that Mr Script from the other day, talking to Mr Fields. What is he doing here? This time he's not alone either. He's got a child with him, all dressed in the purple and gold-edged uniform of Harlan Prep School, and between them, they're holding a scenery board.

"Oh, sorry, we didn't mean to disturb you. I was just explaining to Mr Fields here that we're dropping off some props and scenery to help out." Mr Script smiles **sweetly**. "Shall we bring them in for you?"

"That's very kind of you,

Bill, but I think I did say last time, we're okay and
we don't need any help," Miss Jive answers, coming
to the front of the group.

"Oh, well that's good." Mr Script smiles but it's
a weird tight smile like he doesn't really **mean** it.
"I just thought you can't have too much scenery.
I suppose we can drop this off at the charity shop.
Someone less fortunate can benefit from it."

"Um, I'm not sure people go into
a charity shop looking for scenery
boards," Manny points out.

Mr Script replies curtly, "We're just trying to do a nice thing. Miss Jive here hasn't had the best luck with productions in the past."

Miss Jive looks like she wants the ground to swallow her up and I sense Mr Fields glaring at the Harlan Prep teacher.

Mr Script ignores this, takes a quick look around and then practically **pushes** his way past us into the hall.

"How's your feline cast member doing?" he asks, looking around.

"She's fine, thank you," Milo replies quickly.

"Anyway, we won't keep you, Bill," Miss Jive says urgently. "You must have a million things to do."

Mr Script looks annoyed but keeps talking. "You know, I hear the talent scout is looking for something truly **special** this year, so don't feel too bad if you don't win. We really do have the better facilities at Harlan Prep and...well, it's not your fault that you don't."

Suddenly I realize why Mr Script seems so familiar. The child accompanying Mr Script leans forward and whispers to me just then. "Miss Jive must be the **unluckiest** teacher ever. When she was at our school, she was always having disasters. They used to call her **Jittery Jive**."

That name...I've heard that before!

"What did you say?" I hiss. "Jittery Jive?"

The other kid snaps back, "No, you misheard. Concentrate on the fact that your school has no chance of winning the drama-academy place anyway. Losers!"

Mr Graft steps in and frowns at Mr Script. "Yes, well, Bill, posh facilities aren't everything. Team spirit can take you a long way. Now I'm sure you're busy, so we won't keep you."

Mr Script puts on an extra big smile. "Yes, of course. We'll let you get on with your little production. **Good luck!**"

Miss Jive looks like she might throw up when

he says that. He notices and does a **dramatic** gasp. "Oh dear, what am I thinking? Break a leg, of course, darling, break a leg."

As they walk out of the hall, Milo nudges me. "He said that on purpose, didn't he? Anyone who loves the theatre knows you never say **good luck**."

"Definitely," I agree. "I thought he was okay the first time I met him. Molly seemed to think so too but now I'm not so sure." I go to the door and watch as Mr Script and his minion walk away. The minion turns, sees me watching and pulls a face at me.

Miss Jive, Mr Fields and Mr Graft all head backstage, talking amongst themselves.

I turn to Milo, Mindy and Manny. "I know who's been messing with our musical," I say.

"What? Who?" Milo asks me.

"You know that kid who spoke to me – I've heard his voice before..." I say.

"When?" Milo, Mindy and Manny all ask at the same time.

"You remember on Monday after school when I heard voices in the hall – a man and a child being unkind about Miss Jive? They used the phrase, '**she's always having a disaster**' and they called her '**Jittery Jive**' and laughed. That kid just now from Harlan Prep – that's exactly what he said about Miss Jive and I'm sure the man's voice I overheard must have been Mr Script!"

"So, what are you saying, Neesh?" Milo asks. "I get that they don't like our school much, but do you really think they would sabotage our play?"

Just then we hear a scream from backstage. Miss Jive comes out, looking as pale as a ghost. "The costumes. They've **GONE**!" she says.

CHAPTER TWELVE

DISASTER!

We all stand there, speechless. How can the costumes just be **GONE**?

Mr Graft comes out from behind the stage, shaking his head. "I've checked every room back there, they're **definitely** gone." He leans against the stage and puts his head in his hands. "I mean, where could they be? Without costumes, we won't have a chance of winning this competition. The rules clearly state we need to have made costumes, sets, the whole show," he says sadly.

"We can't just give up!" I protest.

Miss Jive looks at me. "We might not have a choice, Anisha. All the costumes and special accessories like Milo's wig – they can't just be replaced within a day! Maybe it's just not meant to be. Mr Script was right, these things never seem to work out for me." She sniffles. "I knew not sticking to the rules of the stage would lead to **bad luck**!"

"Don't listen to him!" I say. "You always tell us to persevere, Miss Jive, even when things go wrong. That's what we have to do now! I was trying to tell you that someone is sabotaging the show. Do you **believe** me now? Someone is trying to ruin our play on purpose. We can't let them win!"

Mr Graft looks at me. "I admire your spirit, Anisha. And it would be a shame to waste all the hard work that has gone into the production already."

Mindy steps forward. "Miss Jive, you believed in me and encouraged me to audition for this part. You said I have a real chance of winning that academy place. We can't give up now. I want to make you and the school proud. It means so much to us all."

I smile. "Mindy's right, Miss Jive. Maybe someone is trying to sabotage our play not because we're **rubbish** but because we actually have a chance of **winning** this thing!"

Milo stands up. "What's that saying? It's not over till it's over? And anyway, nobody broke a leg yet. That's a good thing, right?"

This makes Miss Jive smile. "You are a gem, Milo Moon. You too, Anisha. And Mindy, you're right, you really are very talented and you do have a good chance of winning that place. We can't give up now." Mr Graft passes her a tissue, and she blows her nose and straightens up.

"You're right, children, the show must go on. We do need a plan, though. The costumes going missing is a big blow, but we can work around it. I can talk to Miss Stitch, the textiles teacher from the high school, and see if she has any material we can work with."

"In the meantime, I have some thoughts on who might be behind all these disasters," I say. "If it's alright with you, I'm going to do some research to check my theory."

Mr Graft nods. "Okay, Anisha. You've got this morning to prove to me that someone is trying to ruin our musical. But if you can't come up with any further evidence, I need you concentrating on helping Miss Jive as the director's assistant. Now let's get a move on!" And with that, he walks away.

Just then Mr Bristles sweeps past us with his broom, whistling. Miss Jive puts her head in her hands. "I told him about not whistling – no wonder this play is suffering so much bad luck. If we don't respect the superstitions of the stage, we're definitely **doomed**!" She wanders off, muttering about the mirror she broke last year and the black cat that lives across the road.

I turn to Milo, Mindy and Manny. "Superstitions or no superstitions, someone is **messing** with our play and I'm sure Mr Script is involved. But we need real proof. We can't just accuse a teacher from another school without proper evidence. I think I get the **motive** – he obviously doesn't want Miss Jive or our school to be in with a chance of winning the competition. But I think there might be more to it than that. He's been in and out of the school all week, so he's had the opportunity to cause trouble. Could **he** have taken the costumes, damaged the scenery, the curtain and caused Molly's meltdown with the olives?"

"Okay, Neesh, what's the plan?" Milo asks.

"Gather round," I reply. "Everyone has a part to play. We need to do our background research.

Manny and I can look online for any more information we can find out about Mr Script."

Manny nods. "I've got my tablet in my backpack, I'll go and get it."

"Great," I reply. "Mindy, you and Milo rehearse as normal, but keep an eye out around the stage and backstage for anything **unusual**. I already found the olives, but there could be other clues. You might find something that will prove beyond a doubt that Mr Script has been on that stage recently, giving him the opportunity to plant the glitter, glue and bowl of olives. And remember, we've got the muddy footprint too. I'm not sure how we can get close enough to check his shoes, plus he's gone back to his own school now but you never know, he might sneak back so we should be on the lookout."

"Got it," Mindy says.

"We're on it, we won't let you down," Milo agrees.

"We've got this," I say. "No one messes with our musical and gets away with it!"

CHAPTER THIRTEEN

NOT GIVING UP YET!

A little while later, as the rest of the year group are busy running through rehearsals with Miss Jive, I sit with Manny and his tablet at the back of the hall.

"Okay, what are we looking for?" Manny asks, bringing up the search page.

"Well, Miss Jive used to work with Mr Script, right? Let's start there. See if there's anything on local news sites about their musical productions in previous years," I say.

Manny taps away and soon there's a whole page of search results.

"Ooh, look at that one. It says **HARLAN PREP FAILS TO PREPARE**." Manny points. He clicks on the

link and there's a
picture of a very
upset-looking Miss
Jive with Mr Script
standing next to
her, his hand on
her shoulder. He
looks a bit **creepy**
to me.

HARLAN PREP
FAILS TO
PREPARE

Much Ado About Nothing: Disappointed
drama teachers Mr B Script and Miss J Jive

Manny reads, "Local teacher Miss Jive had her
five minutes of fame for all the wrong reasons when
her first time leading the annual Harlan Prep
production took a terrible turn."

The article goes on to say that Miss Jive was
in charge of the show, but the night before the
performance all the scenery was found **slashed**
to pieces and it was too late to replace it.

"Wow, she really did have a lot of bad luck,"
Manny says.

"Was it luck though?" I reply.

We go back to the search page. "There's another article about Mr Script," I say, pointing it out.

Manny clicks on the link. There's a great big cheesy picture of Mr Script with the strangest-looking cat I've ever seen. The headline says, **OWNER WINS LOCAL PEDIGREE PET CONTEST WITH RARE BREED OF SPHYNX CAT**. It goes on to say Mr Script is one of very few cat owners in the country with this breed.

"You know what this means, right?" I say.

"Um, he likes weird cats?" Manny asks.

"No, he **knows** about cats," I say. "Look, it says he's been keeping cats for twenty years! He even runs a monthly clinic where he gives advice to new cat owners. He would know about olives being similar to catnip. It's proof, Manny!"

CAT KNOWLEDGE = POWER!

"Is it enough, though?" Manny asks.

"It would be good to speak to someone who knows him, but he works at a different school so that's going to be **tricky**," I say. "Although Mr Script referred to our Miss File as an old friend."

Just then Miss Jive comes over.

"Everything okay, children? Before I forget, Anisha, I seem to have misplaced my copy of the script – the bad luck continues, I'm afraid. Would you be able to go to the school office and make a photocopy of yours for me, please? Miss File will help you operate the copier," she says.

"Shall I go now?" I ask seeing an opportunity.

Miss Jive looks at her watch. "Ah, yes, go on then. Don't be too long, though. We need to run through all the songs before lunch today. And hope nothing else goes wrong." She smiles, showing me her crossed fingers.

I take my script and walk to the office. Miss File is there, as always, sitting behind the desk.

"Hi, Anisha lovely, what can I do for you?" she asks.

"I'm helping Miss Jive with the musical," I say. "I need to photocopy this script, if that's okay?"

"Oh, yes, I can help with that. Pass it over and I'll switch the copier on."

Miss File turns on the big machine behind her and it whirs to life. "So, how's the musical coming along?" She smiles.

"Um, we've had a few **hiccups**," I reply. "You heard about the costumes?"

Miss File looks concerned. "No, what happened?"

"They went missing this morning! Everyone's really upset. We've been working so hard."

"How could they just disappear? Have you checked all the backstage rooms and storage closets?" Miss File asks.

"Yes, miss, we checked everywhere. I think someone took them off the school premises," I say.

"Well, all the fire doors are **alarmed**, so if

someone was going to steal something, they'd have to go past me."

"Did you see anything?" I ask hopefully.

Miss File thinks for a moment. "You say the costumes went missing this morning?" She frowns. "You know, just a little while ago, something **odd** did happen. I was working as normal when I saw Mr Script and his children arrive – four of them, I think. They had a scenery board they wanted to donate and I was signing them all in, but then I heard a loud shriek coming from outside. I left my desk and went to see what was wrong. I thought someone might have hurt themselves. I heard the sound again and followed it round the side of the building, but when I got there – **nothing**. There was no one around. I even walked the long way round the building to make sure! It was all very odd. So, I came back to my desk and thought no more of it."

"Hang on, you said Mr Script had **four** children with him?" I repeated.

"Well, yes, I'm pretty sure there were four. I remember wondering why there were so many when they only had one bit of scenery with them." Miss File shakes her head. "I can't believe the costumes are gone. Poor Miss Jive has worked so hard on this play and after everything she went through at her last school she really deserves to do well."

"What exactly did she go through?" I ask. "Mr Script mentioned you were old friends, is that right?"

Miss File looks from side to side. "Well, I shouldn't say really, but you're a trustworthy girl. Miss Jive used to work at Harlan Prep School with that snooty Mr Script. She was his teaching assistant. I used to work as a temp in their school office sometimes. But that Mr Script, he was awful to her. Always **poo-pooing** her ideas. She tried to make suggestions for their drama productions and he'd say no and then use them anyway – but take all the credit as though he'd come up with the ideas himself!"

"That's horrible!" I say.

"He is a nasty piece of work. When I saw him in school the other day, I did think, **Here comes trouble**." Miss File pulls a face.

"So, what happened? Why did Miss Jive leave in the end?" I ask.

"Well, the head teacher at the school said Miss Jive should have a chance to run the summer performance there and she was doing a really good job. Miss Jive is quite **superstitious** as I'm sure you've noticed and when bad things started to happen, she was a bag of nerves by the end. She just thought she had terrible luck!"

"I heard the scenery was ruined the night before the play. Did they find out who did it?" I ask.

"Never, but I'll tell you one thing. Mr Script didn't seem too upset by it all. I don't think he even wanted her to succeed, in case she was better at running the show than him. Anyway, soon after, Miss Jive left that school and came here – and she's done a fine job ever since, if you ask me. Anyway, you shouldn't worry. My sister's husband's aunty is friends with the head of the drama academy and apparently they're very excited about this being our school's first year in the competition, so they're looking forward to our show the most."

"Really? Do you think Mr Script knows that too?" I ask.

"Possibly, dear, it's a small world." Miss File

nods. "Anyway, I've yapped on long enough. You'd better run along, missy! Here's your photocopy."

I go back to the hall, my head spinning with everything I've just learned. My theory about Mr Script is looking stronger and stronger. If only we had the chance to match up the muddy footprint to Mr Script's shoe then Mr Graft would have to believe us.

I'm just about to walk in through the double doors when Milo comes hurtling out and almost knocks me flying.

"Neesh! There you are!"

"What happened, Milo? Has something else gone wrong?" I ask, worried.

"No. Actually, something has gone **RIGHT**! I was rehearsing with Mindy on the stage..."

"And?"

"And...Molly was playing at the back of the stage, messing about with something. I kneeled down to see what she'd found and it was this." Milo opens his hand and reveals a big brass button. It's in the shape of a theatre mask. One half of the face is smiling and the other is sad.

I've seen that button before. I rack my brain, trying to remember, and then it comes to me. "I'm pretty sure Mr Script has a coat with buttons on just like that," I say.

"I was thinking it looks familiar. Are you sure it belongs to who we think it does though?" asks Milo.

"Almost totally sure. And with what Miss File just told me and the stuff Manny and I found online, it's time to report back to Mr Graft!" I say. "I think we've got enough **proof** to show that Mr Script has been sabotaging our show!"

We smile excitedly but inside my tummy does a somersault. **It's not over till it's over.**

CHAPTER FOURTEEN

THE EVIDENCE!

We go back into the hall and Milo rejoins the rehearsals, but the whole time my brain is **whirring**, thinking of everything we now know and how we can expose Mr Script as the one who has been sabotaging the play. I hold the brass button that Molly and Milo found and turn it over in my hand. I have to get everything straight in my mind before we go to Mr Graft. If we don't **convince** him, he'll just dismiss us and then Mr Script gets away with it. He might even try to **sabotage** the play some more! I can't let that happen. This means **so much** to all of us – especially Miss Jive, who deserves not to be sabotaged any more, and Mindy, who really wants to follow her dream.

Thankfully nothing else goes wrong during rehearsals and the play finally seems to be back on track. The choir are actually **in tune** today and the musicians are playing **in time**, sort of. Beena still tries to be the loudest, of course. Miss Stitch, the textiles teacher, and some students are working hard to replace some of the missing costumes and come up with quick-fix solutions. She makes a bow tie for Milo, which he loves, and she whips up a veil for Mindy to wear in the wedding scene out of a bit of old net curtain.

There's one scene that is still causing some problems though – it's where Mindy has to stand onstage alone and sing her solo. She'd already told me she's really **nervous** about singing in front of a whole hall full of people.

"What if I freeze?" she says as she waits her turn to get up onstage. "I mean singing in rehearsal is okay, because everyone's distracted doing their own

things. But on the night they'll actually be listening – and not just them, the talent scout too!"

"I wish you could hear what I hear when you sing," I say. "It's so beautiful. Honestly, just pretend we're not here. You're going to be amazing." I try to reassure Mindy and she smiles but she doesn't look very convinced.

I know I can't do the performing bit for Mindy, but I can give her the best chance of impressing the scout by stopping Mr Script from doing anything else to sabotage our play. While everyone gets on with rehearsals, I go back to my notebook and lay out all the facts I know so far.

✦	The conversation I overheard calling Miss Jive "Jittery Jive", and later identified as Mr Script and his student.
✳	Large crack in ceiling leading to damaged scenery.
☆	Big hole in curtain.
✦	Molly's meltdown – olives found onstage and research into Mr S shows he is a cat expert so would know the effect of olives on cats.
✳	Brass mask-shaped button found backstage proving Mr S has been back there.
✦	Missing costumes – happened just after Mr S and his students were in the building. Miss File said there were four students but we only saw one!

Soon it's lunchtime. This is it – we have to go and find Mr Graft and tell him everything we now know. The four of us – Mindy, Manny, Milo and I – gather in the corridor while everyone else heads to the lunch hall. We pull together and come up with a **plan**.

"Are you ready, Anisha?" Manny asks. "I've got my tablet with those articles."

"I've got the button Milo and Molly found and what Miss File told me. I've written everything down," I say. "It's now or never. I just hope he believes us and agrees to help."

Manny puffs out his chest and puts on a deep voice. "What's this, Anisha? You want me to do what? I'm not running a school of **vigilantes**, you know!"

We all laugh at his bad impression – until Mr Graft appears round the corner. Then we freeze, embarrassed to have been caught out.

"Hmm, not bad, young Manny. The voice needs

to be much deeper though," Mr Graft booms. "Now do you have an update for me?"

"Um, actually I do," I say.

Mr Graft scratches his chin. "You found something out? Tell me!"

"We can't talk here in the corridor, sir. It's top secret," Manny whispers.

Mr Graft smiles and points in the direction of his office. "Shall we, then? Milo, can you ask Miss Jive to come along too, please? I think she should hear this."

Children usually only go to the head teacher's office for one of two reasons. Either they've done something really, really **good**, or they've done something really, really **bad**. We don't fall into either group, so this feels a bit weird. Once Miss Jive has joined us, we all gather round Mr Graft's desk as he leans back in his big leather chair.

"Right, what's this top-secret stuff you've discovered then?" he asks us.

So, we tell him. We start at the beginning of our investigation, with the overheard conversation and how I later realized those voices belonged to Mr Script and one of his students. Miss Jive gasps when she hears what they said. "I am **NOT ALWAYS** having a disaster," she sniffs.

I continue. "Then, when the scenery was damaged, we noticed how the ceiling tiles had been placed in a perfect pile to the side and there was a muddy footprint left behind." I show everyone the piece of paper with the transferred print on it. "Now, I haven't matched this to Mr Script's foot, but I'm pretty sure he has big feet like this. If I could get close enough, I could even prove it."

"Okay, what else have you got?" Mr Graft asks.

"Well, someone cut a **huge** hole in the curtain and then the next thing that went wrong was when Molly knocked the glitter and glue all over the stage," I say. "We thought she was just behaving badly, but it seemed so out of character. Then I found an **olive** on the floor amongst all the mess she'd caused and more olives kicked under the stage curtain."

"Olives?" Miss Jive asks. "There are no olives in any of the scenes in the play."

"**Exactly!**" I say. "Someone planted them there."

"But why?" asks Mr Graft.

"Because olives have the same chemicals in as catnip! It makes cats go all **floopy**!" Milo exclaims triumphantly.

"We discovered that Mr Script is a cat-owner so he would know this," I continue.

"We found lots of information in these articles," Manny says, holding up his tablet.

"Aha, I see!" says Mr Graft. "You've done some research on Mr Script. What else have you found?"

I look at Miss Jive, not wanting to upset her. "Well, we know that Miss Jive used to work with Mr Script and that he wasn't very nice to her," I say cautiously.

Miss Jive looks at me, surprised, and then sighs. "Yes, you're right. I wasn't very happy working at Harlan Prep. Mr Script liked the sound of his own voice, shall we say, and my ideas were never quite good enough. I seemed to have the worst luck there too."

"I don't think it was bad luck, Miss Jive," I explain. "I think Mr Script deliberately **sabotaged** you then and he's doing it again now."

"No! Surely not?" Miss Jive says uncertainly.

"Miss File says he turned up this morning with four children, but when we saw him outside the hall he only had one with him. Where did the **other three** go? Miss File said she got distracted from her desk by a noise outside. And we were distracted by talking to Mr Script. Where were those three other children when the costumes went **missing**?"

"They'd have to have been fast...but I suppose it's feasible," Miss Jive murmurs. "But I can't believe he'd go to these lengths. Does it mean that **much** to him to win the competition?"

Mr Graft listens intently. For once he doesn't interrupt or tell us off for having vivid imaginations. When we're done, he **thumps** his fist down on the desk and says, "This is **outrageous**! How dare he mess with our musical like that?"

"We found his button on the stage and it's very unique. If we could catch him in the act and confront him with that, he won't be able to deny it. And I have a plan," I say.

Mr Graft smiles. "Aha, yes! What is it? I'll help. I'll do anything for my school."

"We want you to pose in **disguise** as the talent scout," I say. "We're going to **accidentally-on-purpose** tell Mr Script that the scout is coming to check out the school before the performance. He won't be able to resist intercepting and interfering!"

Mr Graft grins. "Genius! I'm in!" He stands up solemnly and puts his hand on his chest. "All for one," he says and then looks at us. "And?"

Milo jumps forward, sticking his arm out like he's holding a sword. "And one for all!" He grins.

Mindy groans. "So cheesy!"

Mr Graft glares and Mindy corrects herself. "I mean, **yay**, one for all!"

I chuckle to myself. This is going to be funny.

"I know you mentioned a disguise, Anisha, but it'll have to be a **good** one, otherwise Mr Script will know it's me right away," Mr Graft points out.

"Ah, we've already thought of that," I say. "My Aunty Bindi went to beauty school; she can change your appearance and disguise you."

"I'm not sure I want my face changing," Mr Graft says. "It's a very **distinguished** face."

"It is, sir – but we want to catch Mr Script, don't we?" I remind him.

"Oh, blast! Okay, I suppose a little change won't hurt," Mr Graft concedes.

"Eyebrow tweezing does though," Mindy giggles under her breath. I nudge her to be quiet. We've got to keep Mr Graft on side.

"Right, so it's agreed. I'll get Aunty Bindi to come here early in the morning, Mr Graft. That way we can confront Mr Script and get all that out of the way so the last few hours of rehearsal can be disaster free before the performance at 4 p.m. Let's run through what you're going to say when Mr Script approaches you at the gate tomorrow. You've got to be **totally convincing**. Our play depends on it."

CHAPTER FIFTEEN

UNDERCOVER HEAD TEACHER

From the moment I wake up on Friday morning I am **super** jittery. Mum and Dad are doing yoga in the garden – it looks freezing out there and who does yoga first thing in the morning like that? It's too early for exercise, if you ask me. Granny Jas is sitting down, having her breakfast.

"All set, **beta**?" she asks me.

"I feel sick," I groan.

"Nervous, huh?" She smiles. "You're not going up onstage though, are you?"

"No," I say, "but I'm still nervous. Everyone has put loads of effort into this play. I just want it to go well."

"I know, **beta**, it will be fine. That's what all the rehearsing is for. I know myself how tiring that can be, but it will all be worth it. I'm looking forward to coming and seeing the show this afternoon. Who would have thought our Mindy would be playing one of the leading parts, eh?"

I grin. "She's **SO** good, Granny, wait till you hear her," I gush. "And Milo is **amazing** as Einstein."

"See, so there's nothing to worry about, is there?" Granny replies.

I hug my Granny Jas; she always knows how to reassure me. "Alright, alright," I laugh. "Granny knows best."

"Exactly!" Granny does her fist punch in the air. "Now, let's get you some breakfast. You can't face a big day like this on an empty stomach. I'll make some eggs and toast, granny-style!"

Then I realize what Granny just said. "Um, Granny, what did you mean when you said you know how tiring rehearsing can be? What have you rehearsed for?"

Granny looks **panicked**, as if taken by surprise. "Um, you know, **beta**, past tense, I mean when I was a child, of course!" She laughs **nervously**.

I eat my breakfast and say goodbye to my family, telling them I'll see them at the play later. I walk down to Milo's house, where he's waiting with a very tired-looking Molly in her carrier.

"It's today!" Milo squeals. "I am **SO** excited! Mindy and I were on the phone for three hours last night practising."

"Oh, that's nice," I say, feeling a small pang of jealousy that Milo and Mindy are getting on so well.

Milo must sense it, because he wraps his free arm around me and says, "Don't worry, no one could replace you as my **bestie**!"

"Get off, you big wally," I say, squirming away but secretly pleased.

"Just sayin'!" Milo shrugs, smiling. "Let's get to

school, catch Mr Script and then we can get on with our play and winning that academy place for Mindy. I literally cannot wait to get onstage today."

We're deliberately early again today and go straight to Mr Graft's office, where we find Aunty Bindi, Manny and Mindy already helping him get ready for our big plan. He's leaning back in his office chair while Aunty Bindi lathers his face with a mud mask.

"Ooh, it smells minty!" he says.

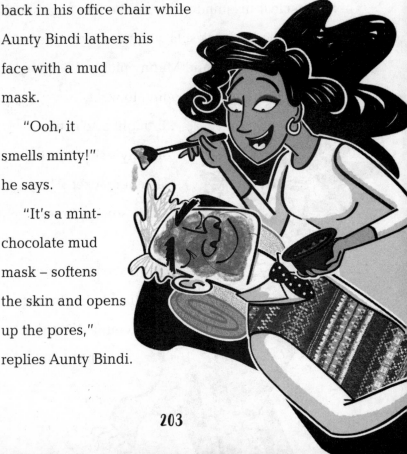

"It's a mint-chocolate mud mask – softens the skin and opens up the pores," replies Aunty Bindi.

"It's lovely. I should do this more often!" Mr
Graft says.

I clear my throat loudly. "Are you sure we've got
time for this, Aunty Bindi? The talent scout is
supposed to be outside the school in half an hour!"

Aunty Bindi looks up. "Yes, yes, don't worry.
This is just a five-minute mask to relax Mr Graft and
help him clear his mind ready for the role he is about
to play. While his mask sets, you two help Mindy
and Manny pick out what he's
going to wear.

I brought a selection
of Tony's shirts and his
leather jacket. There
are some scarves
too."

We go through
the clothes and of
course Manny
and Milo take

the opportunity to play dress-up too.

Mindy tells them off. "Focus, you two!"

"I'm glad you're here to tell them," I say.

"I just want this to go well," Mindy replies. "Do you think it will? I'm already feeling sick about singing later."

"One thing at a time," I tell her. "Let's concentrate on catching Mr Script first – then we can get you ready for your big performance!"

Just then there's a yelp behind us. "**OUCH**! That hurts!" Mr Graft squeals.

Aunty Bindi shrugs. "Your eyebrows needed a tidy. They're so...umm, **distinctive**. We don't want Mr Script recognizing them, do we?"

Mr Graft frowns. "Well, I suppose not. Do be gentle though. Do you really think my eyebrows are distinctive?" he asks as he leans back again.

Mindy and I stifle our giggles as we pick out the clothes. Next Aunty Bindi applies some fake facial hair to Mr Graft's face using special glue which she says will just wash off. You wouldn't think a bit of face fluff would make him look so different. Manny asks if he can try it, but Aunty Bindi says not right now. Then Mr Graft gets dressed behind a screen. He puts on a purple shirt we've chosen, along with the leather jacket and some tight black jeans. We finish the look off with a leopard-print scarf, which he winds round his neck and face, and a big pair of sunglasses.

"Isn't that a bit over the top?" Manny asks.

"Not at all, my boy, I am an ex-star of stage and screen – I am a **chameleon**!" Mr Graft was definitely getting into character!

"We never said anything

about the talent scout being an ex-star," Mindy comments.

"I created a back story; every role needs one," Mr Graft insists, his love of the limelight shining through. "This is going to be the **performance** of my life," he declares.

Miss Jive arrives just at that moment. But she's not dressed in her normal clothes. "Well, I thought why should Mr Graft get to have all the fun!" she laughs.

She's wearing the tree costume from last year's production of **Red Riding Hood** – a brown all-in-one suit which is covered in leaves. She's scrunched her hair upwards so it's curly and wild. Her arms are also covered in leaves. "This way, I can listen in quite close to where Mr Graft will be. There's a tree right there I can lean against. Mr Script will never know!" she says.

Mindy, Manny, Milo and I all look at each other. "Can we dress up too?"

A little while later, Milo and I are hiding out underneath a bench near the school gates, while Mindy and Manny watch everything from inside the wooden hut where all the outdoors equipment is kept. We camouflaged ourselves with streaks of

Aunty Bindi's make-up, though I'm not sure it did much good.

Mr Graft is going to arrive in a taxi any minute, dressed as the talent scout. We wanted it to look convincing so we called a taxi to pick him up from two roads away and sent him walking there to get the taxi back here. Miss Jive told us that there's a new scout at the academy, so Mr Script will never have met them before. **Phew!**

I'm nervous for Mr Graft now though. My tummy is all **wobbly** and suddenly I want to call the whole thing off.

Miss Jive phoned Mr Script last night and pretended to be all nice to him. Then she **accidentally-on-purpose** told him that the scout is coming for a tour this morning at 8.15 a.m. because they heard about how well the play is coming along. She asked him for tips on things the scout might be looking out for, as he's such an expert. That's where our fake talent scout, Mr Graft, comes in. If Mr Script believes all his attempts to ruin our play have failed, he'll definitely want to try and divert the scout. That's our **chance** to confront him.

As we lie in wait, Milo nudges me. "I remembered to bring some stakeout snacks – want some pickled-onion space monsters?" He holds out the packet of crisps to me.

"Um, no thanks, Milo, I had a good breakfast!" I say, trying not to breathe in.

"Do you think Mr Script will really come?" Milo asks while he munches.

"Well, if our theory about him not wanting our school to win the drama-academy place is right, then yes, he'll definitely be here," I say.

"And if not?"

"Well, if not we're back to square one," I say. "But I have a feeling he will. I don't think we've got this one wrong, Milo."

We wait a little longer. A few cars go past. I look at my watch. It's **8.14 a.m**. No sign of Mr Script or

Mr Graft in his taxi. What if Mr
Graft got held up for some
reason? What if Mr Script
doesn't turn up?! I look
over at Miss Jive, who is
pressed up against
a tree. Her
costume makes her
blend into it. She
shrugs as if to say,
I don't know either!

Just as I'm about to
give up, I hear footsteps
approaching. I hold Milo's arm
to stop him reaching into his crisp bag again.

It's him! It's Mr Script! As he comes into view,
he looks around to make sure no one else is about.
Then he waits by the gate.

Milo nudges me. "How much longer? My bum is
going numb!"

"**Shhh!** Mr Graft will be here in a sec!" I whisper.

Right on cue I see the taxi pulling up outside the school. Out steps Mr Graft as the talent scout. He looks around as if he hasn't seen Mr Script standing right there.

"Hello, you must be from the Dreams Dance and Drama Academy. I'm Mr Script from Harlan Preparatory School," Mr Script announces, holding his hand out confidently.

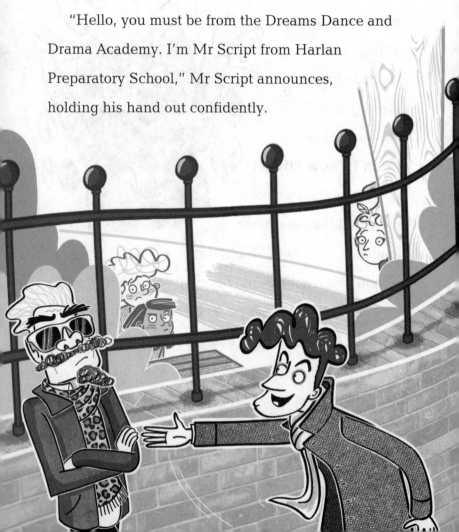

Mr Graft turns to him and says nothing. Mr Script smiles and continues. "I've been sent to look after you. Unfortunately, Aspire Academy have had a **major** disaster, so their play can't go ahead and neither can your tour today. It's very sad, but we at Harlan Prep are more than happy to host you, as we have done your predecessors over the last few years."

Mr Graft finally speaks in a posh tight-lipped voice. "Well, I think I should at least show my face at this school. I would like to see what this disaster is that has struck their production."

Mr Script frowns. "Oh no, honestly, it's probably better you don't see it, they had a major toilet flood and it's all rather smelly!" he lies. "If you come with me, my car is just round the corner and I'll take you to my school. I have some lovely biscuits and we can have some tea in our **LARGE** trophy room. We're a very accomplished school, you know."

"Hmm...I don't know about this. It really

wouldn't be fair of me to just miss this school out of my visiting schedule completely, would it? And I have been looking forward to seeing their production and meeting the teacher – Miss Jive is her name, I think."

"Pah!" Mr Script huffs. "She doesn't know what she's doing! She's an amateur. Not a professional like you and me!"

"Well, it sounds like she's just had a run of bad luck," Mr Graft says. "I mean, that could happen to anyone."

Mr Script loses his temper then. "**NO! NO! NO!** This school doesn't deserve your time! Only my school does! Why can't you see it?" He turns away and starts muttering to himself. "It's unbelievable. That woman was my **ASSISTANT**! **MY** school is the one with all the talent. Not this bunch of losers." Then he swings back to Mr Graft, still determined to convince him. "Did you know they have a cat running riot all over the school? And they lost their costumes only yesterday! A **farce** is what it is! Now, look, you don't need to waste your time here. They're too embarrassed to tell you it's all gone wrong and they don't want you to visit."

We've heard enough. Milo, Mindy, Manny and I jump out from where we've been hiding. "**YOU'RE LYING!**" I shout.

Mr Script spins around to face us. "What? Shouldn't you be in class, children? Run along. This is nothing to do with you."

"Oh, but it **is** something to do with **all of us**," Mr Graft says, flinging off his sunglasses and scarf to reveal his face.

Mr Script squints. "Is that you, Mr Graft? Um...I...er... what is going on here?"

"You've been caught, that's what," I say. "You just gave yourself away by trying to **hijack** the person you thought was the talent scout. You lied about us not being able to show them round today and about our show being cancelled. And you knew about the missing costumes, which you could

only have known about if you were involved in their disappearance."

Mr Script turns red and splutters. "Well, I was doing that for you – to save you the **humiliation**. I heard how badly things were going. I was just trying to help. And Miss Jive, she told me about the missing costumes, she rang me last night, all in a panic."

Miss Jive steps away from the tree, making Mr Script jump. "Yes, I did call you, Bill, but not in a panic at all and I only mentioned the visit by the talent scout – I certainly never mentioned the missing costumes. There was no other way for you to know that. We made sure that piece of information was kept to only a few people in our school."

"See, more lies," I say, folding my arms. "We know it's **you** who has been sabotaging our play. Somehow, you've been sneaking around making things go wrong – and we have proof!"

He looks nervous now. "What proof?"

I pull out the muddy footprint. "I think this belongs to you," I say with confidence. "And this." I hold up the brass theatre-mask button. "I think it goes there." I point to the space on his coat where he does indeed have a button missing.

Suddenly, Mr Script tries to **bolt** away, but Mr Graft is too quick and grabs the end of his long coat. For a second Mr Script continues running on the spot, but he can't get away. He gives up, exhausted, and sits down on the pavement.

"I just wanted to **win**. If Miss Jive started winning the drama-academy places, then next it would be awards, and then what would be left for my school?"

"That's very selfish," Milo scolds. "You should want to see your friend succeed. You're a **BAD** friend!"

Mr Script looks sad and then starts sobbing. "I'm so sorry. I never meant for it to go this far."

Miss Jive sighs. "Oh, Bill," she says. "You never did know when to stop." She shakes her head sadly. "You know it's not just me you were hurting. You were ruining the children's hard work too. They haven't done anything to you and neither did I!"

"I know, I know." Mr Script wrings his hands.

"Bill, this is very serious!" Mr Graft warns. "You made a mess of school property, stole costumes, and damaged the ceiling in the dressing room. Did I miss anything?"

Milo pipes up. "And you used my nan's cat!

The worst crime of all! How could you?"

Mr Script grimaces. "I'm so **ashamed**. I love cats; I have two. I'm very sorry."

Miss Jive frowns. "Really, what have you achieved by doing all this?"

Mr Script smiles bitterly. "You're a **great** drama teacher, Jenny. I should have told you that more often. I was **jealous**, it's as simple as that. I don't have all the ideas you have and I knew the drama academy was interested in you. But that's not your fault and I should never have tried to stop you from succeeding. I'm so **very sorry**. I'll do whatever I can to make this up to you," Mr Script promises meekly.

"Yes, you will. And you can start by showing us where the costumes are!" Mr Graft tells him.

Miss Jive turns to Milo and me. "Right, children, no time to lose, we've got a show to get ready for! We've got just seven hours till the curtains open!"

CHAPTER SIXTEEN

THE SHOW MUST GO ON!

As Mr Graft goes to retrieve the stolen costumes with
Mr Script, we all work together to get the stage
ready for a day of rehearsals. The big performance is
only a few hours away and there's a lot to do. There's
still quite a lot of glitter floating about, so we sweep
and polish everywhere. We arrange the furniture
onstage and line up the props needed for each scene
backstage.

"Do you think we can still pull it off?" M

asks me.

I think for a second. "Miss, in the I

had a ceiling cave in, a flooded dres

destroyed scenery, a holey curtai

in glitter, missing costumes, and Molly going floopy. And we're still rehearsing. We all still want to put on this show. I know we can do it."

Miss Jive smiles. "Do you know what you've got, Anisha? A very important quality – determination. You never give up and I really admire that about you."

I blush. "Thanks, miss."

So, we get to work. We have a last run-through of the play from the start and it looks great. I'm just thinking, **Phew, we're back on track**…and then we get to Mindy's solo. I knew she was nervous about performing in front of all the grown-ups and the talent scout, but when she comes out for her scene she looks as pale as a ghost.

"Are you okay, Mindy?" I call out.

"I feel…umm…a bit queasy," she manages to say ore she runs offstage towards the toilets.

go," I say and follow Mindy to the girls'

She's splashing some
water on her face when
I walk in.

"I can't do it,
Anisha. I just
can't!" she cries.
"I'm sorry, I know
everyone has
worked so hard and
you went to all that
trouble to find out who

was sabotaging the show, but I
just can't do that solo in front of the talent scout."

"Okay," I say, remembering how Mum says
sometimes you have to let people work stuff out for
themselves.

Mindy eyes me suspiciously. "Is that reverse-
psychology stuff? I won't change my mind, you
know."

"Okay," I say again.

"There's no point trying to convince me," Mindy says firmly.

"I won't then," I respond.

"**Urgh**, Anisha, stop being **infuriating**. Say what you really think. I know you want to!" Mindy almost shouts.

"Look, you're really **talented**, that's all," I say. "It would be a shame not to show everyone."

"But what if I'm rubbish? What if I forget the words? What if I'm out of tune!" Mindy exclaims.

"Yeah, I get it. But what if you don't?" I point out. "What if you're **brilliant**?"

Mindy smiles. "You're a pain, Anisha Mistry. Why do you have to **believe** in people so much?"

I grin. "Only the ones **worth** believing in."

"Argh, okay, I'll try. I can't promise I'll be good though, and I can't promise I won't throw up with nerves just beforehand." She frowns.

"I'll keep a bucket at the side of the stage," I say, holding the door open for her.

As we make our way back to the hall, the rest of the school is buzzing with excitement. All anyone is talking about is the show. We pass a Year Three kid saying, "Did you hear there's a real-life cat in the play? How awesome is that?" and it makes me smile.

Miss Jive is busying around the hall, checking this and that. She spots us returning and gives us a **thumbs up**. "All okay?"

Mindy blushes. "Yes, miss. It was just a bit of nerves. I'll be okay."

And so, we get back to work, finishing the run-through and making sure everyone knows what they're doing.

We've decided everyone in the choir and all the dancers should wear the same bow tie as Einstein, so that's about **forty** ties to be put on, which takes longer than you think. They do look amazing when they're all done though.

Milo looks so great as Einstein. I help him adjust his wig.

"Neesh, it's really happening! Don't tell anyone, but I'm wearing my lucky pants – they never fail! Do I look okay?" he asks, grinning at me with his classic Milo smile.

"You look **great**," I say, feeling so proud of my friend.

"How about me?" asks a voice. I turn around and it's Mindy. She looks fantastic as Mileva. Her hair is parted in the middle and pulled back in a low bun. She's wearing a dress with a big frilly collar and a locket around her neck. She looks totally convincing. **"Wow**, Mindy!" I say.

"You are going to blow everyone's socks off!"

"Ha, I hope not! I had enough of Milo's bare feet, I can't take a whole roomful!" jokes Mindy.

Soon it's time for the performance. Half an hour before the show is due to start, I stand in the wings, just left of the stage, and tawke a second to look at what we've achieved. The set looks amazing. There's a section in front of the stage either side for the choir and the musicians to sit. The stage is dressed like Einstein's house with a kitchen table and all his papers spread out on it. The scenery that Ava and Ayesha repainted looks awesome. Manny and Govi managed to create some extra backgrounds with some old boards Mr Graft found too. Everything looks so good.

Just then Miss Jive brings someone over to meet me. "Anisha, this is Janice, the scout from the drama academy," she says excitedly.

"Hi."

"Hello, I've only been here five minutes and I've already heard so much about you," Janice smiles. "I understand you have been an enormous help to Miss Jive."

I blush. "I don't know about that."

"I do!" Miss Jive interrupts.

"Well, I'm very much looking forward to watching the musical. It sounds **fantastic**." She looks around. "Now, where can I get a cup of tea?"

"I can help with that!" says Mr Graft, coming up to us. "I have a stash of chocolate biscuits too, but don't tell anyone!" And off they go, chattering and laughing together.

Miss Jive gives my arm a squeeze. "The scout seems lovely, doesn't she? I really hope she likes our show. But you know what? Even if we don't win, you're all superstars to me."

Time goes by so quickly and backstage is bustling with activity as we put the final touches to make-up and hair, and place props into the right hands. I stand just behind the curtain backstage. Thankfully Miss Stitch had time to patch up the holey curtain too. I look out into the audience as all the children, teachers and parents file into the hall. There's murmuring and shushing as everyone settles into their seats. Mum, Dad, Uncle Tony, Aunty Bindi and Granny Jas get great seats in the front row, right next to Janice and Mr Graft. They spot me and give me little waves and thumbs ups and I can see Aunty

Bindi getting right in there, introducing herself
to Janice.

Suddenly there's no more time to worry or
prepare. The lights go down. Everyone falls silent.
This is it.

CHAPTER SEVENTEEN

IN THE SPOTLIGHT!

The spotlight comes on and Mr Graft walks onstage. He thanks everyone for coming and then finally the show begins. The musicians take their places at the side of the stage and start to play the intro. There's a bit of a false start when they do their first piece and someone drops their guitar and it makes an almighty **clang**. But like true professionals, they carry on and it works out okay. I watch, almost holding my breath in the wings.

Everyone cheers when Milo makes his entrance. With his wig and cardigan, he looks so much like Einstein! Molly is by his side and is just perfectly **paw-some**. I'm so proud of them. When Mindy makes her entrance as Mileva, they light up the stage together. I swear even Beena is smiling as they do the song about Einstein's love of sailing and not being able to swim.

Mindy is **dazzling** and totally convincing as Mileva. When it's time for her solo, she looks over at me, takes a deep breath and just sings. Her voice is

so beautiful that when she finishes everyone stands up to clap. Aunty Bindi jumps up cheering and making wolf-whistle sounds while Uncle Tony weeps and shouts, "That's my baby!"

Mindy looks a bit startled but then breaks into a wide smile and even looks a bit proud of herself. I clap so hard my hands hurt.

For the first time the whole play goes totally to plan. Even the scene where Milo and Mileva get married – finally, after all the bickering, I watch them and believe they are happy to be doing it! The choir are in tune, the musicians are on the beat and the dancers are twirling in the right direction. There are no forgotten lines and everyone is where they're meant to be, at the right time. It's a stage-show **miracle**!

At the end, when the cast do the final song all about the wonder of science and the power of dreams against the backdrop of the starry scenery, I feel quite emotional. I turn to look at Janice and my family. Mum and Dad are beaming. Uncle Tony is still weeping. Aunty Bindi is jumping up and down and Granny Jas is telling everyone, "My granddaughter, Anisha, helped put this play together."

I catch Janice's eye and she gives me a huge thumbs up. She liked it!

Everyone onstage takes a bow and then another. The curtain closes and the cast start to leave the stage, but then it opens again! The cast have to run back on, but Milo trips and his wig comes flying off, landing on Beena's head. She does not look amused but the applause in the hall is deafening, so she just smiles through gritted teeth.

And through all the laughing and cheering, I just keep thinking, **We did it, we really did it**.

After the hall has pretty much emptied and most of the cast are getting changed or have already gone home with their parents, our family is busy talking to Janice. I sit on the stage with Mindy, Milo and Manny and we talk about how amazing it's all been.

"Milo, you were **brilliant**!" Mindy tells him.

"Er...**YOU** were **AMAZING**!" Milo replies.

"You were both amazing," Manny says. "You too, Anisha – it wouldn't have come together without you."

"We **all** did it," I say. "Everyone played their part. The scenery and the props looked so realistic, Manny! You and Govi did such a great job."

"Anisha is right," Janice says as she walks over to us. "It was an immense team effort. I have never seen a year group work so well together."

We all look at each other and burst out **laughing**.

"You wouldn't think that if you'd seen us a few days ago," Milo admits.

"Well, you came good on the day, that's all that matters," Janice insists. "And there is some real **talent** here. I'm looking at you, Mindy."

Mindy blushes. "Me?"

"Yes, you. You have such a pure, wonderful voice. Which is why I'm delighted to offer you the academy place. We could do with a voice like yours for our summer production!"

Mindy gasps. "**I won?**"

"Yes. Well, I still have other schools to see but it's my choice if I think we can offer more than one place. Anyway, I definitely want to offer you a fully paid scholarship place at our academy next summer. Congratulations!" Janice confirms. "Of all the school plays I've watched so far today, not only has this been the best one, but you, my dear, have just blown me away."

We all hug Mindy. This is so **incredible**.

"You know, Anisha, if you want to come and do some work experience at the academy, we can always use a resourceful, determined pair of hands on our shows. Plus, your Aunty Bindi has just offered to run a Bollywood class for us. It looks like we'll be getting the whole family involved," Janice says with a smile.

I don't know what to say, so I stand there with my mouth open. I realize I would love to do it. I always thought Science and Maths were my thing but I've really enjoyed being part of the production. It might be fun to spend some time at the academy next summer!

Manny nudges me. "Say yes, you'd **love** to," he whispers.

Janice chuckles. "It's okay, it's a lot to take in. I just want you all to know how **impressed** I was by the show and your efforts in keeping it going against all odds. Mr Graft told me you'd all had some setbacks but you didn't give up. That perseverance will serve you well when you're older."

We say our goodbyes and once Janice has gone we just stand there, taking in what has just happened.

Manny suddenly **snort-laughs**. "You know what this means, right? If Bindi is going to run a Bollywood class at the drama academy, she's going to want to try it out on us first!"

Mindy **groan-laughs**. "Oh no, you're right."

Miss Jive comes over then. "I hear congratulations are in order, Mindy!" she says, high-fiving us all. "You are all **fantastic**, I want you to know that. Now scoot, before I cry again! Your parents are all at the main entrance."

Everyone grabs their bags and starts to leave. I hang back and turn to Miss Jive. "Thanks, miss," I say.

"Whatever for?" Miss Jive asks. "You all did the work!"

"Yes, but you taught us to persevere even when things go wrong. And to try things outside of our comfort zone and to believe in ourselves. I just want you to know we – I mean, I – really appreciate it," I say.

Miss Jive's eyes fill up. "Thank **YOU**, Anisha Mistry, because you reminded **ME** to do all of those things too."

CHAPTER EIGHTEEN

DIWALI DOUGHNUTS

The next day is the weekend and it's **DIWALI**!
After the week we've had at school, our house seems
quite normal, which is saying something.

Milo joins us, as he does for every big family
occasion. He's basically a Mistry anyway. He wisely
leaves Molly with his mum to take back to his nan's
house. "Nan will be missing her," he says.

Granny Jas brings out all her **amazing** food
and we eat till our tummies feel like they might
explode. There are three kinds of chicken,
lamb curry, spicy vegetable curry, rotis, puris,
four kinds of pickle, pakora, dhokla, patra,
samosas, gelebi, gulab jaman, penda, ras malai

and what's this at the end? Doughnuts?**

"Doughnuts, Granny?" I ask, confused.

"Ah, they didn't have my nice mithai at the sweet centre. All sold out by the time we got there. If Bindi had taken me earlier like I asked, instead of spending three hours adjusting the lights, it would have been okay – but no, we didn't get there till 1 p.m. and it was all gone! So, Bindi suggested we get these doughnut thingies with the sprinkles on them."

"Yummy!" Manny says through a mouthful of cream-filled doughnut.

"I think it's fine, Granny. Doughnuts are good, too!" I laugh.

* My granny makes so many delicious treats! I think she could make her own cookery book except she doesn't like to measure ingredients: it's always a pinch of this or that. Anyway, pakora are a fried snack made with gram flour wrapped around potato, onion and spinach – so yummy! Dhokla look like little yellow sponges. I could eat a whole plate of them! Patra are one of Granny Jas's specialities, they're made with a special kind of leaf and gram flour. Granny makes the best samosas too, fried pastry wrapped around spicy meat or vegetable, so good! And then the sweet stuff, gelebi, gulab jaman, penda, ras malai, I love them all. How many puddings is too many?

"Happy Diwali, bete. I'm so proud of all you kids," Granny says, pulling me in for a hug. Mindy, Manny and Milo all pile in too. Mindy's dog Bella barks and jumps up, trying to join in.

"Careful, you'll squash Granny!" Dad warns.

"Nonsense!" Granny says. "I'll never be too old and fragile for a hug from these four."

We're still hugging when Aunty Bindi jumps up and says, "C'mon, I've got a surprise for you all outside."

I groan. "Oh no, not another light switch-on?"

"No! Actually, something even better." Bindi winks. "Come on, it'll be worth it, I promise."

So, we wrap up warm and go outside…

Wow, I was not expecting this!

We all let out a little gasp as we see the most magical scene in our garden. Aunty Bindi has lit what feels like a thousand candles and she's got the outdoor heater on, so it **almost** feels cosy. (Almost.) She's assembled a little stage area with a draped covering and fairy lights all around it. "Sit down," she urges us and disappears behind the stage with the other grown-ups.

We all squish up on the patio sofa and wait, wondering what's going to happen. Suddenly there's sitar music and Aunty Bindi's voice narrates: "A long time ago in a faraway land, there lived a princess called Sita."

Mindy nudges me. "She's doing the story of Rama and Sita, isn't she? How they fell in love and then got banished and then there was that big battle with Hanuman and Ravana!"

Just then Aunty Bindi steps out, dressed in a beautiful red and green sari. She's got a gold tika on her head.

"I think so," I whisper back. "So, this is what all the dodgy behaviour was about the other day! I'm guessing Aunty Bindi is going to be Sita."

Mindy groans and puts her hand on her face. "That means Dad will be Rama! Cringe! If they smooch, I'm leaving. I'm telling you now!"

I chuckle, glad it's not my mum and dad doing it. But then as the story goes on – **horror of horrors** – Mum steps out and starts joining in as an evil queen who wants to banish Rama and Sita. Uncle

Tony as Rama is quite funny – he's got blue face-paint on to make him look like Rama in that picture Granny Jas has of all the Hindu gods. But he's jumping around so much being a brave warrior that he's sweating and now his face just has streaks of blue running down it.

Then Dad comes out, playing the part of the evil king Ravana! They've obviously been rehearsing as well. He kidnaps poor Sita and takes her away to his castle. Aunty Bindi really lays on the drama here, wailing, "Rama, save me!"

Finally, Granny Jas comes and saves the day as the monkey warrior and god, Hanuman. She befriends and helps Rama and, fighting in a great battle together, they defeat Ravana and save Sita. We all cheer as Rama and Sita find their way home thanks to the lamps the people light for them.

I know we're only in our back garden, but the story and all the divas make it really **magical**. It feels like we're there in the faraway land of Ayodhya, the place Rama is believed to have been born in India.

"I never thought I would enjoy a play with all our parents in it," Mindy marvels.

"Dad was quite good, I thought," Manny agrees.

"You kids were having so much fun putting on your play, it reminded us how much we enjoyed doing such things when we were youngsters," Dad explains.

"And you know I love any excuse to get dressed up!" Bindi grins, holding out her scarf.

"I tell you what, it's **exhausting** being a star of the stage," Uncle Tony says. "I don't know how they do it! I'm out of puff with all that fighting off baddies and then the long walk round the garden."

As it gets colder, Uncle Tony and Dad decide they're in charge of the fireworks. Aunty Bindi stays on standby with the phone in case she needs to call the fire brigade. Uncle Tony seems to have bought the biggest box of fireworks he could find – it's bigger than him. They go right to the end of our long garden to set them up. Mindy, Manny, Milo and I make a den out of some chairs and some old tarpaulin and camp out under there to watch from safety.

There are a few hair-raising moments when Uncle Tony almost lights the wrong end of a firework and Dad isn't very quick at getting out of the way. Mum says next year we're going to a proper display with health-and-safety marshals – this is too stressful!

"Nonsense!" says Dad. "This is how my dad did it in the old days."

"Oh, Bhagavan!" Granny sighs. "Don't remind me! Well, we're not in the old days any more, and you can either do it safely or not at all!"

Dad pouts but does as he's told.

I look around at my family and the fireworks

exploding in the sky. All the colours light up our faces – blue, yellow, pink. The air crackles around us and for once we are all quiet, just watching and enjoying – it doesn't happen very often! Right at this moment, I feel very **lucky**.

We're not perfect and stuff goes wrong around us **A LOT** – but we always work it out and we always have each other. We make a great team.

After such a hectic week at school, part of me would love to believe that tomorrow I can just read my book in peace and nothing weird or mysterious will happen. But the realistic part of me knows:

MISTRY FAMILY
+
ANY SITUATION
=
MISTRY CHAOS!

ACKNOWLEDGEMENTS

Publishing four books in two years feels strange and overwhelming. I've basically been wondering how I got here the whole time to be honest. The team I work with are phenomenal and I wouldn't be writing books without them. Kate Shaw, my wonderful agent. My amazing editors Stephanie King and Alice Moloney, who breathe life into my words. Katarina Jovanovic, Stevie Hopwood, Sarah Stewart, Will Steele, the whole team at Usborne and of course the brilliant and mega talented Emma McCann. Team Anisha continues to support and sprinkle magic on this series with so much love and care and I couldn't ask for a better publishing home.

To teachers everywhere, you have my heart. If ever we understood and appreciated how important you are in shaping and nurturing our children it has been in the last two years. Thank you for all you do, not least encouraging a love of reading in and outside of your classrooms.

Booksellers, librarians, bloggers and reviewers, my continued and endless gratitude for giving my books your support.

Thank you to the author community for love, reassurance, calm, celebration in the good times and general mood lifting when it gets tough.

To the readers, you make my dream real. I can never thank you enough. I hope Anisha's adventures continue to make you smile.

And to anyone thinking about reaching for that long-held dream, do it. It's got to be worth a try and it could turn out to be the most amazing thing you ever do.

My children, my nieces and nephews. You are my why. xx

MEET THE AUTHOR

Name: Serena Kumari Patel

Lives with: My brilliant family, Deepak, Alyssa and Reiss

Favourite Subjects: Science and History

Ambitions: To learn to ride a bike (I never learned as a kid).

To keep trying things I'm scared of.

To write lots more books.

Most embarrassing moment:

Singing in Hindi at a talent show and getting most of the words wrong. I hid in the loo after!

MEET THE ILLUSTRATOR

Name: Emma Jane McCann

Lives with: A mysterious Tea Wizard called Granny Goddy, a family of bats in the attic, and far too many spiders. (I promise I'm not a witch.)

Favourite thing to draw: Spooky stuff like Dracula's Den in Anisha's first adventure. (Still not a witch, honest.)

Ambitions: To master a convincing slow foxtrot.

Most embarrassing moment:

I used to collect old teacups and china. One day, I was in a teashop with a friend and the cup she was using was really pretty. I picked it up to check the maker's mark on the base, forgot it already had tea in it, and spilled the lot all over the both of us. (Witches are too cool to ever do anything like that.)

Look out for the fifth fantastic mystery from

ANISHA

ACCIDENTAL DETECTIVE

HOLIDAY ADVENTURE!

"Pack your bags – we're off to a holiday camp! Milo can't wait to see the wildlife, Manny's learning survival skills, and even Granny's going to have a go at archery. Honestly, I just want to read my book, but there's NEVER any time to relax for Anisha, Accidental Detective. The holiday park's mascot, Delilah the duck, has been DESTROYED, and my new friend Cleo is everyone's number one suspect. But I'm sure she's innocent, and I'm going to do whatever it takes to prove it. Let's hope we can find the real culprit and QUACK the case!!"